The Wobbly Life

of Scarlett Fife

ILLUSTRATED BY CHRIS JEVONS

HODDER CHILDREN'S BOOKS

First published in Great Britain in 2022 by Hodder and Stoughton

1 3 5 7 9 10 8 6 4 2

A CIP catalogue record for this book
is available from the British Library.

ISBN 978 1 444 95777 8

Printed and bound in Great Britain by
Clays Ltd, Elcograf S.p.A

The paper and board used in this book
are made from wood from responsible sources.

Hodder Children's Books
An imprint of
Hachette Children's Group
Part of Hodder and Stoughton
Carmelite House
50 Victoria Embankment
London EC4Y 0DZ

An Hachette UK Company
www.hachette.co.uk

www.hachettechildrens.co.uk

The Wobbly Life of Scarlett Fife

Also by
MaZ EVanS:

Who Let the Gods Out?

Simply the Quest

Beyond the Odyssey

Against all Gods

Vi Spy: Licence to Chill

Vi Spy: Never Say Whatever Again

Vi Spy: The Girl with the Golden Gran

And look out for more books
about Scarlett Fife:

The EXPLODING LIfe of Scarlett Fife
The STORMY LIfe of Scarlett Fife

For Arf

Who stops my Worry Wobbles.

But can make wobbly very fun.

Love ya, bestie

xxx

Scarlett

Maisie

Polly

Ms Pitt-Bull

Aunty Amara

Aunty Rosa

William U and his mum

Emmeline

Jakub

Unimingo Power!

Gran

Rita

Bruce

ChapteR 1 X 1

Families are a bit like polygons (*'polygons', by the way, is a posh word for 'shapes'. I learned that in Year 4 and made my old teacher Mrs Funn snort her tea when I said that Mr Bitt's new haircut was 'an interesting polygon'*). Polygons (*and families*) can be lots of different shapes.

You can have a family that has three parents and one child, like mine, which is like a square:

You can have a family that has two parents and one child, like my worst enemy in the whole world, William U's, which is like a triangle:

His mum

His dad

William U

(*William U has left my school, St Lidwina's, which is THE BEST NEWS EVER! William U's mum decided after Christmas that What Upset William was our school and everyone in it, so she moved him to a private school. A private school, by the way, is one that you pay for. It's not private like the staff room is private and children aren't allowed in, which makes sense, because it would be a shame if children weren't allowed inside their own school after they'd paid all that money.*)

Sometimes you can even have a family that has two parents and fourteen children, like my Granny Nancy's family, who came from Wales, which is like a hexadecagon (*Ms Pitt-Bull told me that, by the way, when I asked what a sixteen-sided polygon is called, which is why she's my teacher and I'm on The Purple Table for Maths*).

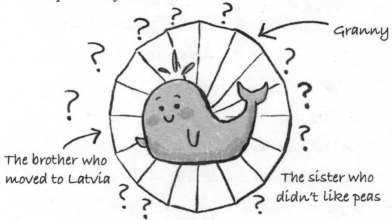

Granny

The brother who moved to Latvia

The sister who didn't like peas

(*Granny's family came from Wales the country, by the way, not whales that live in the sea. That makes sense, but I used to hope I was part whale so I'd be able to swim without goggles one day.*)

But families aren't exactly like polygons, because polygons don't change their shape and families change shape all the time.

Families can change shape for good reasons, like my BFF Maisie's foster family, which sometimes welcomes new children and sometimes gives children to their Forever Families. Maisie is still waiting to find her Forever Family, but her foster family has been lots of different polygons:

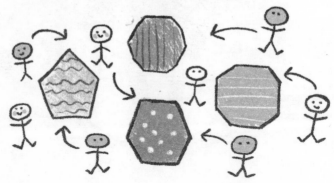

Then they can change for sad reasons, like my not-friend-not-enemy Polly's family; her daddy died two years ago. There aren't any two-sided polygons, but I think families with one parent and one child (*or two grown-ups, like my Aunty Rosa and Aunty Amara*) are like a circle:

1) because I can see their arms joined together like a hug

and

2) because I can't think of any other shapes that work

Then sometimes families change shape for reasons you're not sad about, but you're not happy about either.

My dad's girlfriend is Rita. Rita is Polly's mum.

My dad really likes Rita. They've been going out for three months now (*which is quite a long time for my dad, by the way*) and Dad keeps trying to join Polly's circle to my square.

I don't know what polygon that would make. But I know I have **BIG FEELINGS** about it (*like when Dad invited Rita and Polly on our special 'just us' trip to the ice-cream parlour and my quintuple choco-marshmallow sundae blew up, because sometimes stuff explodes when I get angry **BIG FEELINGS**, by the way.*

I don't want to join Polly's circle to my square. I like my square how it is. I still don't know how I feel about Polly. But I do know this:

I don't want Polly in my polygon.

I just want Polly gone.

Chapter 3 – 1

Tonight we are having a Family Dinner. This isn't unusual – every few weeks we all get together at Aunty Rosa and Aunty Amara's Big Posh House or a Restaurant With Colouring and spend Quality Time Together, which means that all the grown-ups stop spending time on their phones in different places and instead spend time on their phones in the same place.

But what is unusual is that tonight we are having a Family Dinner at my house. And what's even *unusualler* is that my mum is cooking it. And what is the most *unusuallest* thing of all is that we're all looking forward to it because MY MUM HAS LEARNED TO COOK!

It's amazing! For the past few weeks she's been making all this actually yummy food that actually tastes like it's actually supposed to! It's bad timing though, because Mum is on some weird diet and she never wants to eat anything – everything makes her feel 'A Bit Queasy' (*which means she needs to puke, by the way, but Granny says it's more polite to say 'A Bit Queasy', just like she says 'Passing Wind' when she means farting, or 'Backside' when she means bum, because that's what they said in the olden days. Granny also has Polite Olden Days ways for saying wee and poo, so she talks about 'Spending a Penny' and 'Having a Number Two' which I think sounds like she's ordering a really cheap takeaway*).

'Isn't it funny?' I say as Granny and I sit down for the delicious-smelling Actual Roast Chicken Mum is making. 'Now *Mum* feels sick when she eats her food, when before *we* all felt sick when—'

Granny smiles and puts her hand over mine,

which is her Polite Olden Days way of saying 'Be Quiet Now'.

'What?' says Mum, looking like she's going to cry. She looks like she's going to cry a lot at the moment – and for once I know it's not her cooking that's the problem. 'What? What have I done?'

'Nothing, darling,' says Granny, smiling at Mum and holding my hand quite formidably (*my granny is really formidable, by the way, which means that everyone does what she says*). 'Smells wonderful.'

'Hi, Nancy,' says Jakub, coming in from the garden. 'I didn't hear you arrive. I was just clearing out the compost heap.'

Jakub is at home a lot at the moment because he's still looking for a job. After Nasty Gary gave him the wrong sort of sack from his cleaning job, Jakub has been trying to find a new one. But until he gets one, he is also working really hard at our garden, which he loves, and it's looking really pretty.

Mum says Jakub has Green Fingers, which is weird because they're usually brown from all the mud.

'Look at the state of my floor!' says Mum, looking like she's going to cry again at the one muddy footprint Jakub has left by the back door. 'It's TOTALLY RUINED!'

Jakub gives Mum a big hug.

'I'll clean it up, Emi,' he says, giving her a kiss. 'That chicken smells delicious.'

'Well, it won't be delicious for long,' Mum sniffs. 'If Rosa and Amara don't get here soon, it'll be TOTALLY RUINED!' (*Mum thinks lots of things get TOTALLY RUINED, by the way. The hall carpet was TOTALLY RUINED when I wore my wet wellies one step off the doormat. Her new dress was TOTALLY RUINED when she spilt a drink on it, even though the drink was water. And her whole life was TOTALLY RUINED when we ran out of kitchen roll, which she needed to clean the hall carpet and her new dress.*)

'Sorry we're late!' shouts Aunty Rosa, bursting through the door, with Aunty Amara floating in behind her. 'Got held up at work.'

Aunty Rosa grins at Aunty Amara.

'We have something to tell you.' She smiles. 'We are—'

'Well, I have something to tell you too,' says Mum, interrupting her little sister. 'But it'll have to wait. Because this roast chicken will be TOTALLY RUINED if we don't eat it now.'

'It's so lovely of you to cook, Emi,' says Aunty Amara, giving Mum a big hug and some flowers. 'Thank you so much for having us.'

Mum takes the flowers. And then she starts actually crying.

'This ... you ... you're so ... they're so ... I'm so ...' Mum sniffs, snotting over her flowers, which will actually be TOTALLY RUINED if she gets bogeys all over them (*Granny doesn't have a Polite Olden Days way of saying 'bogey', by the way. I don't think they'd been invented when she was younger.*)

'So what's your big news?' Jakub asks Aunty Rosa as he pours the grown-ups a glass of wine.

'Well,' says Aunty Rosa, 'I found out today that—'

Suddenly there's a big crash at the other end of

the room. We all spin around to look – Granny is face-down on the floor. Seeing her there makes me feel A Bit Queasy – is she hurt?

But Granny is never hurt. She is formidable.

'Stop fussing,' says Granny formidably as Jakub helps her into a chair. 'I just tripped over, nothing to panic about.'

I look over to where Granny fell over. There's nothing to trip over. Maybe 'tripping over' is a Polite Olden Days way of saying something else.

'Now,' says Granny, taking a sip of her wine. 'What's this big announcement?'

'OK,' says Aunty Rosa, looking over at Aunty Amara. 'So I've been talking to my boss and—'

'Oh no,' says Mum, suddenly looking really pale. 'I think I'm going to ...'

She runs out of the kitchen before she can be A Bit Queasy all over the floor.

Aunty Rosa sighs and looks at Granny.

'You sure you're OK, Mum?' she says seriously.

'I'm absolutely tickety-boo,' says Granny, which is another Polite Olden Days way of saying 'Be Quiet Now'. 'So how are you, Scarlett? How's school?'

'It's OK,' I shrug. 'We've got a new head teacher starting this week.'

'Another one?' says Granny. 'What happened to Miss Pelling? She's only been there five minutes.'

'Miss Pelling went to a conference about The Importance of Stable Leadership,' I explain.

'What happened?' asks Aunty Amara.

'Dunno,' I shrug. 'She never came back.'

'So who's your new Head?' Aunty Rosa asks, filling Granny's glass with not as much wine as Granny wants.

'He's called Mr Calling,' I tell her. 'He's going to make St Lidwina's a Centre of Excellence.'

'Good,' says Granny, drinking her wine.

'Children should strive to be the best.'

'But children also need to learn about themselves, about each other, about the environment,' sings Aunty Amara, dancing on the spot. 'Those are excellent too.'

'Not if you're trying to get a job,' huffs Granny, who went to school in The Olden Days when they made you get a job when you were about eleven.

'But what is "best"?' says Aunty Amara. 'Maybe you're the best at being a good friend? Maybe you're the best at trying hard? Maybe—'

'This is such an interesting conversation,' I say, because I'm totally bored and need to say something.

'Sorry, everyone,' Mum apologises, walking in with a tissue in one hand and Jakub in the other. 'But we've got some news ...'

'So have we,' interrupts Aunty Rosa, rushing back to the table before Mum can get there. 'As I was just about to say before you ran off—'

'Now now, girls,' sighs Granny, putting a hand to her head. Jakub moves her wine away. 'Let's not quarrel.'

(*That means 'fight' in Polite Olden Days.*)

'I was here first,' Aunty Rosa says.

'No, you weren't – I live here!' snaps Mum.

'Why don't we all try to guess the good news!' grins Aunty Amara. 'We could make it a game with riddles and songs ...'

'Will you just let me speak!' shouts Aunty Rosa.

'Will you just be quiet and listen!' shouts Mum.

'WILL YOU SIT DOWN AND BE QUIET BECAUSE THERE'S PLENTY OF TIME TO HEAR FROM BOTH OF YOU!' shouts Granny, standing up and banging on the table.

Now, that was formidable.

Both Aunty Rosa and Mum sit down quickly.

'Right,' says Granny. 'As you are both behaving like children – sorry, Scarlett – then I will treat you like children. If you can't take turns, then no one gets to go first.'

'But—' Mum starts.

'Emmeline!' Granny warns. She used Mum's big name. Mum's in big trouble. Aunty Rosa knows it and sticks out her tongue.

'Rosa!' Granny warns again, and Mum folds her arms happily.

'Now,' says Granny. 'Why don't you both tell us your news at the same time? That way no one is first and we can celebrate both pieces of news at once.'

Mum and Aunty Rosa both sulk, but they don't disagree. Granny is so awesome.

'Right ... on the count of three,' Granny begins.

17

'One ... two ... three ...'

'We're moving to New York!' Aunty Rosa shouts.

'We're having a baby!' Mum shouts louder.

'What ... wait ... what?' I burble. Suddenly a strange wobbly sensation starts up in my tummy. It's sort of tickly and sicky all at the same time. I think it's another **BIG FEELING**. A worried **BIG FEELING**. And I don't like it at all.

'You're moving to New York? In America?' says Granny, looking confused and happy and sad all at the same time. 'But ... why?'

'I've been offered a promotion in our New York office,' smiles Aunty Rosa. 'It's a great opportunity.'

'And we want a big adventure,' says Aunty Amara. 'And what better adventure than a new life in a new country?'

'Wait a minute,' I say. 'So ... Aunty Rosa and Aunty Amara are moving to America? But that's ... that's ages away. And Mum's doing what ... ?'

Mum looks at me with a big, teary smile. Jakub comes up behind her and rubs her tummy.

'Scarlett.' Jakub smiles at me. 'You're going to be a big sister.'

The Big Wobbly Feeling grows bigger in my tummy. This is all very worrying. A baby? But ... that changes our polygon. With a baby, we're ... we're going to be a ... pentagon. I don't want to be a pentagon. I want to be a square. I like my square. Why is everyone trying to change my family's shape?

My Worry Wobbles are getting stronger. But everyone's looking at me like they want me to be really happy. I don't want to make my family sad. But my aunties all the way across the ocean in New York? And a pentagon baby ... ?

I force out a smile as the Worry Wobbles work their way up my body. Maybe the smile will let them out.

A strange movement catches the corner of my eye. It's Mum's roast chicken. It's starting to wobble, like it's trying to belly dance (*a bit like my dad did last week in his kitchen and Rita laughed so hard she choked on a salt and vinegar crisp*).

'Are you OK, Scarlett?' Mum asks, looking like she's going to cry again.

I think about what to say. I'm not feeling OK at all. But I don't want to upset Mum. I look over at Granny. What would she say?

'I'm absolutely tickety-boo,' I answer, trying to

keep the smile on my face as I watch the belly-dancing chicken. I think about the new baby and losing Aunty Rosa and Aunty Amara and how much I really need to Pass Wind right now and the Worry Wobbles get bigger and the chicken is belly-dancing all along the kitchen counter now, any minute now it's going to go ...

PLLLLLLLLLLOPPPPPPPPPP!

The wobbly chicken wobbles off the side and on to the kitchen floor, making a noise like it just Passed Wind and did a Number Two all at the same time.

My Worry Wobbles stop as I stand there in shock, looking at the splatted chicken all over the floor.

Oh no.

Is it happening again? My angry BIG FEELINGS make things explode. Do my worried BIG FEELINGS make things wobble? No. It must just be a coincidence. There's absolutely nothing wrong with—

'MY CHICKEN!' says Mum, running to the chicken on the floor. 'It's TOTALLY ...'

21

She kneels down to tidy it up. But before she can finish, she immediately gets A Bit Queasy and runs out of the room again.

Aunty Rosa goes over to the splatted chicken and picks it up. She wipes off a leg and chews on it.

'It still tastes better than her old cooking,' she whispers with a wink.

Chapter 9 ÷ 3

'But it'll be fun to have a baby brother or sister,' Maisie says. 'Just think – a whole new person to love.'

Hmmmm.

It's science time in Rainbow Class and we're doing an experiment to see what makes an egg float. Ms Pitt-Bull says school is to prepare us for life, but when I asked her when in our lives we're going to need to make an egg float, she told me to be quiet and concentrate on my work. And I need Maisie's red-glasses perspective on this new baby. (*Maisie wears red glasses, by the way, and I think they help her to see things in a clever way. And they're just really cool.*)

'Maybe,' I say, poking my egg with a spoon. 'But Mum and Jakub could have asked me first.'

'I've got two little brothers and they're both rubbish,' says Vashti, whose egg is sinking. 'They break all my toys and they're always snotty.'

'My little sister sleeps in my bedroom and she always farts,' says Millie.

I feel a Worry Wobble in my tummy. I hadn't thought about that. Where is this baby going to sleep? Mum and Jakub have a bedroom and I have a bedroom. We don't have any more bedrooms. Maybe the baby is going to sleep in my bedroom?! I don't want a snotty, farty baby in my bedroom!

'When the stork brought my baby brother Thomas, I got loads of presents,' says William D. 'I asked if the stork could take Thomas and the set of encyclopaedias my Uncle Stan gave me back and leave the other presents behind, but my mum said we had to keep them all.'

The Worry Wobbles stop. Presents? Presents are good. But I can still get presents at birthdays and Christmas without having a snotty, farty baby in my room.

'Storks don't bring babies,' says Polly, butting in on our conversation (*Polly always butts in, by the way. I think it's because her mum drives an ambulance*). 'Parents make them.'

Polly thinks that just because her mum drives an ambulance, she knows everything about the human body.

'How?' Maisie asks. 'How do parents make a baby?'

Maisie always asks good questions. I hadn't thought about that either. How did the baby get in Mum's tummy in the first place?

'When two people love each other very much,' Darcy says, 'they wish on a magic star and they get a baby. My dad told me.'

25

'No, they don't,' says Roshin, whose egg is floating (*Roshin is really good at science, by the way*). 'Babies aren't magic. They are biological. You get them by sharing your toothbrush.'

'That's rubbish,' says Felix. 'My dads made me with my Aunty Becky, so I know all about how babies are made. You need an egg and a seed. You mix them together and you get a baby.'

We all look at down at our eggs. Suddenly everyone bursts out laughing. Felix says the funniest things. What does he think we are? Chickens?!

'Felix is right,' says Polly, getting her egg to float as well. 'My mum told me all about it – and she drives an ambulance.'

(Polly is always going on about how Rita drives an ambulance, by the way. It's super annoying.)

'You're telling me that someone has to lay an egg

to have a baby?' I snort, holding up my egg. 'Well, I'm not putting an egg in *my* tummy.'

'Actually, you've been born with all the eggs that you need to make babies,' says Polly smugly. 'So you've already got loads.'

I look at the egg in my hand, then down at my tummy. Where am I keeping all these eggs? I feel full enough when I have one on toast.

'Rainbow Class!' says Ms Pitt-Bull, shaking the Attention Tambourine. 'Please bring your experiments to my table and come and sit on your carpet spaces. We are going to have a Special Meeting to welcome our new head teacher, Mr Calling.'

An excited whisper goes around the class. We've had eight head teachers since I started at St Lidwina's in Nursery. We always have a Special Meeting when they come and then another one when they leave. Twice now, they've been on the same day.

We all put our eggs on Ms Pitt-Bull's table and she puts them high up on her bookshelf out of the way (*which is probably a good idea, because Milly is always breaking stuff, like the time she sat on Parva's model of the Tower of London that Parva had made from her recycling and Parva cried so hard she got to sit in the Quiet Corner with a special book about wizards all afternoon*). I pass Mr Nibbles (*who is our class hamster, by the way*) and stroke him. We had so much fun together at Christmas so I'm working really hard to get lots of Positivity Points to be Star of the Week and get him back again. Maisie and I sit next to each other on our carpet spaces.

'I'm really not sure about this new baby,' I whisper to her. 'What if I don't like it?'

'You don't have much choice,' Maisie sighs, cleaning her glasses. 'Your mum is pregnant. So ipso lactose, that baby is coming.'

'What does that mean?' I ask.

'It's Latin for "you don't get any say in it",' she explains. (*Maisie is so clever with words, by the way. Last month she entered a competition on the radio to write a 500-word story and she came third out of EVERYBODY, so she got to go to London and win an iPad from someone who used to be in a soap opera. It was super cool.*)

The door opens and a young man walks in. I wonder if he's a student – sometimes they come from the university to practise being a teacher with us (*like the one who came when we were in Year 3, by the way, and told us we shouldn't be taught in classrooms but outside in the forest where we can climb trees and make fires. He only came that one day. I hope he's having fun in the forest*).

'Mr Calling,' Ms Pitt-Bull announces. 'This is Rainbow Class.'

I look around to see our new head teacher. But there's no one other than this student.

'Well, thanks, Ms P-B,' says the student with a really big smile. 'But I think – no, I KNOW – you're wrong on both counts.'

Ms Pitt-Bull raises an eyebrow. This student is going to go on the The Cloud for making bad choices if he's not careful.

'Firstly, I'm not Mr Calling,' grins the student. 'I'm Trent.'

We all look a bit confused. Nice to meet you, Trent, but we're here to welcome our new head teacher.

'If I'm going to call you by your first names,' Trent continues, 'then I want you to call me by mine. So call me Trent. No Mr Calling here.'

Again, Trent, that's great to know – but where is he?

'In fact, I'd like all my staff to start using their first names,' says Trent, smiling at Ms Pitt-Bull, who is not smiling back. 'I read a study that said

using first names creates empathy and equality. So what can the children call you, Ms Pitt-Bull?'

Ms Pitt-Bull raises her eyebrow again.

'Ms Pitt-Bull,' she answers.

'O-K!' laughs Trent, raising two thumbs and winking. Felix raises his hand.

'Great – a question already!' grins Trent. 'Go!'

'Er ... do we call you sir?' Felix asks. 'Because that's what we called our last head teacher who was a man.'

I try not to laugh. First Felix thinks that people lay eggs and now he thinks this guy is the new head teacher! He's so funny.

'Uh-uh – no way!' cries Trent. 'When I get a knighthood, then you can call me sir. Until then, your head teacher is called Trent!'

'So our head teacher is called Trent too?' I ask Maisie. She rolls her eyes behind her red glasses.

'Trent IS our new head teacher,' she says.

Um ... WHAT?!

This is our head teacher? But he's not old enough!

'Now, the other thing I need to correct Ms Pitt-Bull about is who I have in front of me,' he says. 'When I look around this room, I don't see Rainbow Class. No! I see ... POTENTIAL!'

We all look around. Trent might be young but he needs my glasses – we're all right here in front of him.

'That's right, guys. I believe – no, I'm CERTAIN – this is a room FULL of potential!' says Trent. 'YOU are full of potential! And as your head teacher, I promise – no, I VOW – I'm going to find it and unlock it inside each and every one of you!'

I look at my tummy again. I don't know if I've got room for any potential inside me with all those eggs.

'I think!' Trent shouts, making Ms Pitt-Bull startle. 'No – I BELIEVE – that St Lidwina's is a world-beating school! So let's beat the world! I'm delighted – no, I'm HONOURED – to announce that at the end of this term, St Lidwina's Primary School is going to SET A NEW WORLD RECORD!'

Everyone gasps and starts chattering. Ms Pitt-Bull just raises an eyebrow.

'Yeah!' says Trent, nodding and pointing his fingers. 'We are going to set the new world record for ...'

I think of all the records in my world record book. Are we going to be the fastest? The loudest? The tallest?

'... stacking sugar cubes!' Trent cries.

Oh. That's fun too.

'The current record stands at 2,669 cubes,' Trent continues. 'And I believe – no, I'm CONVINCED – that we can beat it. From now until the end of term, we are going to practise stacking sugar cubes.

Then in the last week of term, an official world record judge will watch us beat – no, SMASH – that world record!'

Everyone starts clapping and cheering. This actually does sound quite fun.

'But we're not just going to beat world records,' says Trent, opening his arms. 'St Lidwina's is going to beat – no, DEMOLISH – all the other schools in the area. Ms Pitt-Bull, who are your two best mathematicians?'

'We don't use the word "best" in Rainbow Class, Headmaster,' says Ms Pitt-Bull. 'We celebrate all our different abilities.'

'And I don't use the word "Headmaster", Ms Pitt-Bull,' laughs Trent, raising his thumbs and winking again. 'But allow me to rephrase – who has the differently best ability in Maths?'

Ms Pitt-Bull's eyebrows go up again.

'Polly,' she says wrongly. Polly puffs up like her mum's ambulance has just pulled into the classroom.

'Great – come to the front, Dolly,' says Trent. Polly loves going to the front. This is so stupid. It's not fair to pick people out for special treatment when everyone should get an equal chance to—

'And Scarlett,' says Ms Pitt-Bull.

Actually, now I think about it, this is a really good idea.

'Come on up here, Charlotte,' says Trent with his big grin.

'It's Scarlett,' sighs Ms Pitt-Bull.

'I thought you were Ms Pitt-Bull,' says Trent, laughing at his own joke. I don't think Ms Pitt-Bull wants to put Trent on The Cloud. I think she wants to put him in Rita's ambulance.

I walk to the front of the class and face all my friends.

'Rainbow Class?' Trent announces. William D puts his hand up.

'Yes?' Trent answers.

'I thought we were called "Potential" now,' says William D. 'And do you like dinosaurs?'

'You ARE Potential!' says Trent, laughing at William D, who is now very confused. 'And as for dinosaurs, I like them – no, I LOVE them – but I don't wanna be one! I want St Lidwina's to be modern – no, CUTTING-EDGE – no—'

'The best at stacking sugar cubes?' Vashti says.

'No!' cries Trent. 'I want St Lidwina's to the best at EVERYTHING! I value every single one of you as special individuals with your own unique identity. And that's why Dolly and Charlotte here are going to represent our school at MathsQuest, the regional Maths competition! So say it with me, everyone: '*Go, St Lidwina's! Go, St Lidwina's!*'

Everyone starts clapping and cheering. Polly and I just look at each other. Represent the school? In a big Maths competition? That's ... that's ... that's ... really scary.

I can feel the Worry Wobbles in my tummy again. I love Maths, but doing it in front of other people ... that's terrifying. What if I get all the answers wrong? What if I let the school down? What if everyone laughs at me? What if I Pass Wind and all my eggs fall out? What if ... ?

I look above Trent's head at Ms Pitt-Bull's bookshelf. All the eggs are starting to wobble. Everyone's going really hyper now, stamping their feet and cheering with Trent. I watch the eggs wobble and wobble as I think about MathsQuest and the snotty, farty baby and all the eggs in my tummy and Aunty Rosa and Aunty Amara moving to America and the Worry Wobbles get worse until they feel totally out of control so I just close my eyes and ...

SPPPLLLLLAAAAATTTT!

All twenty-nine eggs (*there should be thirty, by the way, but Freddie is having his adenoids out*) wobble off Ms Pitt-Bull's bookshelf and splat one by one on to Trent's head. He tries to keep talking, but it's quite difficult with eggs splatting on your head.

'So [*splat*], what I [*splat*] want everyone [*splat*]

to take from [*splat*] today [*splat*] is the importance [*splat*] of taking eggsellence [*splat*] – I mean excellence – [*splat*] very, [*splat*] very [*splat*] seriously [*splat, splat*].'

Everyone stops clapping and cheering and starts laughing. Ms Pitt-Bull picks up the Attention Tambourine and shakes it.

'Rainbow Class! Rainbow Class, calm down, please!' she tries to shout over all the noise. But no one's listening. They're all laughing too hard.

But I'm not laughing as I look at all the mushy eggs dripping down Trent's head. First Mum's roast chicken. Now the eggs ...

Oh no.

That's it.

Looks like I've got a new **BIG FEELING**.

And this one is going to cause me even more Big Problems.

CHAPTER 2 X 2

I have a lot to talk to my dad about tonight.

'That's a huge honour!' he cries when I tell him about MathsQuest. 'I'm so proud of you! I can't wait to come and cheer you on! Now – how did Rita show me how to make that omelette last week? It was so good ...'

I try to smile. The thought of Dad in the MathsQuest audience makes me feel even wobblier.

'Dad?' I ask as he starts to get my omelette ready. 'How did you put the seed in Mummy?'

'Sorry?' he says, ducking down into the saucepan cupboard.

'The seed?' I tell him. 'The one you used to make me. How did you get it into Mum's tummy?'

Suddenly all the saucepans clatter to the floor.

'Ah ... well ... er ...' says Dad as he picks them up. 'What ... How much do you know already?'

'Too much,' I sigh, thinking of all the eggs in my tummy. I hope they're free range.

'I see,' says Dad, carrying the pan to the stove. His right arm is wobbling (*my dad was born without all his left arm, by the way, which makes his right arm super strong so he can lift me up and spin me around for five minutes or until I puke*). That pan must be very heavy.

'But what I don't know,' I continue, 'is how your seed made me?'

Dad looks like he doesn't know what to say. I'm surprised he doesn't know more about this stuff.

'So ... well ... you're bound to be curious with the new baby coming,' says Dad, pacing up and down the kitchen. 'And this is an important conversation and one that should be addressed with honesty and clarity.'

'OK,' I agree.

'And so ...' says Dad, taking a deep breath.

'Yes?' I reply.

He shuts his eyes like he needs a Number Two.

'And so ...' he repeats.

'Go on,' I say. Now he looks A Bit Queasy.

'So ... so ...'

'YES?!' I cry. He's making this very hard work.

'So ... Go and ask your mother,' he burbles, going back to his cooking. He looks super embarrassed. I think I know what's going on here. No wonder Dad's blushing.

He can't remember how he did it.

Just like the omelette.

'Oooh, can we watch *UniMingoes 4Eva* tonight?' I ask him (UniMingoes *has been made into a movie, by the way, and it's the BEST movie EVER! I'm not sure if Dad agrees yet, but I think he'll enjoy it more after the fifteenth time we've watched it together)* .

'Um, not tonight, sweetie,' says Dad.

Oh no.

Sweetie. That's never good.

'Why not?' I ask him cautiously.

'Well, I thought it might be fun ...' he begins.

Double Oh No.

Let me explain something:

There are things my dad knows:

1) Any song from the 1990s (*although it's quite easy when the words are just MMMBop*)

2) Why the referee is wrong (*and what he had for lunch – it's always pies*)

3) How to hoover (*my dad is just really good at hoovering*)

But there are things that my dad doesn't know:

1) How to do hair (*he thinks a pony tail is a story about a horse*)

2) Why kids' TV is so much better now than in The Olden Days (*this one show, by the way, they put a bucket on someone's head and made them walk around a room with their friends shouting at them! If we did that, we'd be put on The Cloud*)

3) What is actually fun (*not Differently Fun, like some adults think*)

Things that Dad thinks 'might be fun' include: tidying my room, watching football (*which makes no sense if the referee is so wrong and just thinking about pies, by the way*) and lately, the thing he always thinks is fun ...

'... if Polly and Rita came over,' he says.

I knew it. So I pull a face to prove it.

'Oh, come on, Scarlett,' he says softly. 'Don't be like that.'

'I'm not being like anything,' I say, pulling another face, which also isn't being like anything.

'I just ... I just think that it would be nice for you to take the time to get to know Rita and Polly,' he says.

'I already know Polly. I spend every day with her at school,' I say, rolling my eyes, which isn't being like anything either.

'Well, maybe if you spent time out of school with her—'

'I've already got to do MathsQuest with her!' I say loudly, but not at all being like anything. 'And I like it when it's just you and me.'

'So do I,' says Dad. 'But when you go back to Mum, it's just me. And I'd like to have someone then too.'

I get a funny feeling in my heart. I haven't really thought about what Dad does when I'm not there. I just sort of thought he ... waited for me to come back again.

'Please, Scarlett,' he says, looking at me with sad eyes. 'Please try. For me.'

I sigh, which is the last thing I'm going to do that isn't being like anything.

'OK,' I say. 'But we watch *UniMingoes 4Eva* this weekend?'

47

'Twice,' he grins, putting the omelette down in front of me. I stare at it. I feel a bit differently about eggs after today. I used to think they just came from chickens. But now I have to be more careful.

'Don't tell me you're not hungry?' he says. 'I had to get those eggs especially.'

'How?' I ask suspiciously.

'I ran out this morning,' he smiles, putting my juice down next to me. 'So I had to borrow these.'

'Who from?' I ask suspiciously.

'From Rita,' says Dad. 'Luckily, she had loads.'

I push the omelette away. I'm not hungry any more.

The doorbell rings and Dad leaps to get it. I hear Rita in the hallway. Polly shuffles into the kitchen.

'Hi,' she mutters.

'Hi,' I mutter back.

She sits down at the table with a face like a dropped egg.

48

'This wasn't my idea,' she says. 'I wanted to stay at home and watch *UniMingoes 4Eva*.'

I pull a face and snort a bit like that was a really silly idea.

Dad and Rita go quiet in the hallway. That usually means they're kissing. Dad and Rita kiss ALL the time. They cannot keep off each other. It's like Rita's a fridge magnet and my dad's face is the fridge door.

'Eugh,' says Polly.

'Eugh,' I agree.

'Look,' she suddenly whispers, leaning across the table. 'I've been thinking. I don't want my mum with your dad ...'

'Well, I don't want my dad with your mum,' I say to make it even.

'I knew that,' she says (*Polly always has to be right about everything, by the way, it's super annoying*). 'So we need to work together.'

'To do what?' I ask.

'To break them up,' she says, like it's super obvious.

'I knew that,' I point out, because I'm right. I usually am.

'You know your dad, I know my mum. If we can make them find out things about each other that they don't like, between us we must be able to figure out how to split them up.'

I try to think of a reason that this isn't a good idea, but I can't.

There's no need to say it out loud though.

Dad and Rita's voices start up again in the hall.

'Are you in?' Polly asks.

I nod. I want my dad back. I need to protect my polygon.

'Hey, Scarlett,' says Rita with a big smile. 'Huge congrats on MathsQuest. That's amazing!'

I smile back as the Worry Wobbles start up in

my tummy again. Why is everyone making such a big deal about MathsQuest? I just want it to go away.

'Our girls,' smiles Dad proudly, putting his arm around Rita. 'What a team.'

Polly and I look at each other like the other one just Passed Wind.

Rita sits down as Dad puts the kettle on.

'So, Scarlett,' Rita asks, being all friendly and nice and smiley. It's super annoying. 'What do you think of Trent?'

'I think we'll be having another Special Meeting quite soon,' I say.

Rita laughs a big, happy laugh. Polly looks shocked.

'That's so funny,' Rita giggles. 'That's exactly what Polly said!'

I look at Polly and she looks at me. That was just a coincidence. I'm nothing like her.

'So, girls,' my dad starts as he comes to the table with Rita's coffee. 'Rita and I have been talking ...'

They both giggle and kiss each other AGAIN (*kissing should be like saying hello, by the way. You should only be allowed to do it once per conversation*).

'... and,' Dad continues, 'we thought it might be fun ...'

Oh no. I roll my eyes. So does Polly. That's two coincidences (*which is also just a coincidence, by the way*).

'... if we all went away together!' says Rita, finishing Dad's sentence (*they also do this a lot. In the 2.6 seconds their mouths aren't busy with all the kissing*).

Polly and I look at each other and pull the same A Bit Queasy face. That's just a coincidence to add to all the other ones.

'Where?' Polly asks, sounding like they've just announced we're going to the dentist.

'To Kamp KwalityTime!' Dad announces, doing jazz hands, as if that ever made anything better.

'Kamp KwalityTime ... is that the place on the telly where it's always sunny and there's horses and a swimming pool and everyone laughs when they're eating and you can book your magical escape today for a low, low deposit, terms and conditions apply?' I ask.

'That's the one,' Rita giggles, kissing my dad YET AGAIN. 'Polly's wanted to go for ages, haven't you, Pol?'

Polly makes a noise that could have come from her mouth or her Backside.

'And you've been talking about us having a holiday for ages, Scarlett,' says Dad, putting a shiny brochure on the table. Polly and I both look at it. There's a family on the front who are smiling in the sunshine as they ride horses and swim. They must be really happy about their low, low deposit. It actually does look quite fun ...

'We just thought,' Dad starts, putting his arm around Rita, 'that it would be a great chance for us all to get to know each other a bit better.'

'I think it's a great idea!' Polly suddenly says

brightly, looking straight at me. 'I bet we'll find out all kinds of things about each other on this trip.'

She nods and I nod back to show I understand her meaning perfectly.

(*I don't understand her meaning at all, by the way, but she doesn't need to know that.*)

'When Elizabeth's mum from Rainbow Class went on her first holiday with her new boyfriend,' Polly says sweetly, 'they split up because he chewed with his mouth open. She dumped him over his table manners.'

'Ha!' says Dad, quickly sticking out his pinkie as he drinks his coffee. 'Well, I'm sure we'll be fine, Polly. Your mum is so laid-back, it's great ...'

'... and your dad is up for anything,' says Rita, smiling at him. 'It's one of the things I enjoy most about him.'

They both giggle and kiss again. I want to puke up Rita's eggs I didn't eat.

55

'Hey – before I drop you back to Mum, why don't you girls go and watch *UniMingoes 4Eva* while we ... clear up in here,' says Dad, holding Rita's hand.

'It takes two of you to put two cups in the dishwasher?' I ask.

Dad gives me the 'Don't Be Like That' look.

'Come on, Scarlett,' says Polly, picking up the brochure and dragging me into the other room. 'Let's leave them to their cleaning up.'

She pulls me into the living room, switches on *UniMingoes 4Eva* so the adults can't hear us and starts to whisper.

'Don't you see?' she says excitedly. 'This is it! This is our chance!'

'To watch *UniMingoes 4Eva*?' I say. 'I'm sure if we'd just asked—'

'No – not that, dummy! If we can show your dad and my mum each other's bad sides at Kamp KwalityTime, they'll break up!'

'I knew that,' I say, because I obviously did.

'OK – so Mum says she likes your dad because he's up for anything,' she says. 'What won't your dad do?'

'My hair?' I suggest.

'No – something we can do at Kamp KwalityTime,' Polly says. 'What's he afraid of?'

'My granny?' I think out loud. 'Ooooh – and heights. He won't even climb a ladder.'

'Good to know,' grins Polly, flicking through the brochure. 'Lots of opportunities here.'

'What about your mum?' I ask. 'Dad said she was really laid back.'

Polly bursts out laughing and hands me the brochure.

'Yu-huh,' she says sarcastically, 'until she gets super competitive. Don't ever play a game with her.'

I flick through the brochure looking at the family playing all kinds of competitive sports together.

I don't know if they're applying the terms and conditions, but they seem happy enough.

'There are loads of games here,' I say.

'Perfect,' smiles Polly. 'My mum hates losing. We have a plan.'

We both smile at each other.

But then we stop because that's just weird.

I look around the room. It's gone quiet next door. They're probably ...

'They're probably kissing,' grumbles Polly, which wasn't at all what I was going to say and not another coincidence at all. 'What are we going to do?'

We both look at the screen, where the UniMingoes are singing about how everyone is special, especially if they buy a limited edition 'I love UniMingoes' hoodie.

'I'll watch it if you really want,' I sigh, really hoping she does.

'Yeah, OK,' says Polly quickly, running to the sofa and sitting down just in time for the UniMingoes to go on their adventure. We both laugh as OopsieMingo falls over like he always does.

(*Which, by the way, is just another coincidence.*)

ChapTER 20 ÷ 4

Tonight we're at Aunty Rosa and Aunty Amara's Big Posh House because:

1) Mum says she wants to talk to them about moving to America without chicken all over the floor.

2) She wants to use their Big Posh Kitchen because it's got a Bigger, Posher oven than ours.

3) Jakub has been here since Very Early to do some gardening for them.

4) It's a really nice, Big Posh House.

None of us is happy about Aunty Rosa and Aunty Amara moving to America. My mum has been discussing loads of reasons with Jakub about why my aunties should stay and she's written them out on different-coloured pieces of paper so she can make a good argument. I'm just going to sit here and sulk until they change their mind.

'But it's all so sudden. When will you go?' Mum asks as she gently places the final chocolate egg on top of the chocolate nest on top of the three-tiered chocolate cake she's making (*Trent is challenging all the parents to The Great St Lidwina's Bake Off, by the way, and Mum is entering an Easter cake. It actually looks like a proper grown-up cake and everything, not like the time she baked cupcakes for the Valentine's Day bake sale and Charlie S in Reception's stepdad bought them because he thought Charlie S had made them*).

'Just after Easter, when all the paperwork is ready,' says Aunty Rosa, sipping her wine. 'It's a good move for us. There's lots of work for Amara in America, I'm getting a big promotion and we want to get settled before we start a family.'

'You want to start a family?' I ask, forgetting to sulk.

'Of course,' says Aunty Amara, kissing my head. 'Why wouldn't we want someone like you to love?'

'Well, you'll need to find some seeds,' I sigh as Mum takes out her phone to take a picture of her cake.

'Who ... thinks ... Charlie S ... made ... this!' Mum spells out as she presses the buttons on her phone.

'What's that, squidge?' says Aunty Rosa.

'If you want to have a baby,' I explain (*how do none of the grown-ups know this stuff, by the way?*), 'you need eggs and seeds.'

My aunties just look at me as Mum's phone bleeps a new WhatsApp message. Mum starts to look A Bit Queasy.

'Well,' says Aunty Amara. 'There are lots of ways to make a family. Some people make babies themselves, others make a family through surrogacy, fostering or adoption.'

'I know – like Felix and Maisie's families,' I point out. 'But if you want to make a baby yourselves, you're going to need a seed.'

Aunty Rosa looks over to Mum, but she's busy with her phone.

'Yes,' says Aunty Amara, smiling. 'You're right, we would.'

'Well, if you need any seeds,' I point out, 'you should ask Jakub. He's got loads.'

Aunty Rosa spits her wine across the table and starts laughing.

'He does!' I tell her. 'They're in his shed – you can go and ask him if you don't believe me.'

'I believe you, squidge,' says Aunty Rosa, wiping her mouth. 'Don't ever change ...'

'Oh no,' says Mum, tapping away at her phone. 'Charlie S is Rory's brother from Rainbow Class. Melissa is going to think I was being rude about her son when actually I was joking about my baking.'

'What's that, Emi?' asks Aunty Amara.

'The Rainbow Class WhatsApp group,' says Mum. 'They're all going to hate me.'

Oh no.

The Rainbow Class WhatsApp group. Here we go again ...

Let me explain something:

After Christmas, Emma R's mum thought it would be a good idea for all the parents in Rainbow Class to start a WhatsApp group for Helpful Suggestions. But the only thing it seems to have

Helped is lots of arguments.

Earlier this term, everyone got into loom bands and we were all making friendship bracelets and necklaces and ... really long strings of loom bands. But then on the Rainbow Class WhatsApp group, Misha's mum Helpfully Suggested that Sir David Attenborough had said about the danger of plastic in the ocean and were loom bands really environmentally friendly? I don't know what Sir David Attenborough was doing on the Rainbow Class WhatsApp group, but it meant I had to throw my loom bands away, which I had BIG FEELINGS about because surely loom bands are better on my wrist than in the ocean making mermaids A Bit Queasy?

Then after Rory's party in February, Rory's mum went on the Rainbow Class WhatsApp group to thank Misha's mum for Rory's present (*which was this rhyming picture book we all got in Year 4, by the way, about a clever squirrel who learned it's more fun to go to school than eat sweets in front of the TV – so ... not that clever then).*

Rory's mum put a picture on the Rainbow Class WhatsApp group that showed Rory's 'new' book had already been signed – to Misha. Rory's mum asked Misha's mum if Sir David Attenborough said it was environmentally friendly to recycle your daughter's old birthday presents? So Misha's mum Helpfully Suggested that Rory's mum could be more environmentally friendly by not driving her 4x4 one mile to school – perhaps she could run as she always wears her gym kit anyway? Then Rory's mum Helpfully Suggested back that Misha's mum should wear her gym kit and go running more often, which meant they used Bad Choice Words to each other in the playground at pick-up the next day and Ms Pitt-Bull had to talk to both of them in our classroom.

Personally, I think the Rainbow Class WhatsApp group has caused nothing but trouble. Sir David Attenborough should seriously consider leaving it.

'Who could hate you?' Aunty Amara says to Mum. 'But social media is responsible for a lot of anxiety ...'

'I'M NOT ANXIOUS!' Mum wails, before starting to cry a bit.

'Of course you're not,' says Aunty Amara, coming over and giving her a hug. 'But this is one of the reasons I don't have a phone. That, and I've lost my last six ... What's the problem?'

'I'm trying to organise a night out at the end of term,' sniffs Mum. 'But everyone keeps saying they're busy. Do you think I've upset them? Perhaps I should ask them.'

'No,' says Aunty Amara, taking the phone away. 'You should always treat social media like driving – only do it when you can see clearly.'

'Hi, everyone,' says Jakub, coming in the back door, taking one look at Mum's teary face and wiping his feet properly on the mat. 'Those tomatoes are looking great.'

'Must be your seeds,' says Aunty Rosa, taking a sip of her wine and giggling.

'I nearly forgot, this came for you this morning,' says Mum, blowing her nose on a hanky before handing Jakub a letter with posh handwriting on it. 'It looks official. Who's writing you letters? Are you in trouble? Do you owe someone money? Are we going to get a visit from the police?'

'No, darling, no,' says Jakub, reading the letter and giving Mum a kiss. 'It's nothing like that – it's from Lady Tottington-Snoot.'

'Lady Tottington-Snoot?' says Aunty Rosa. 'The one who owns Tottington Hall?'

(*I know that house, by the way. Aunty Rosa and Aunty Amara have a Big Posh House, but it's nothing*

68

on Tottington Hall – that's like a castle. It sits on a hill at the top of our town. I used to think a dragon lived there. When I told Mum that, she said that I was right. But the only person who lives there is Lady Tottington-Snoot, so I don't really understand where she keeps the dragon.)

'What does she want?' says Mum, looking all panicky. 'Are we in trouble?'

'No, my love,' says Jakub, looking worried. 'She wants me to come and interview for a job!'

'Wow!' says Aunty Amara, taking the letter. 'She says she's looking for a new groundskeeper and has been admiring your petunias as her chauffeur drives her past. She wants you to come to Tottington Hall tomorrow so she can meet you.'

'Way to go, Jakub! Remember your seeds!' says Aunty Rosa, raising her glass, which Aunty Amara takes away with a little kiss.

'Oh no. This is terrible!' says Mum.

'Why?' I ask. 'Jakub's always wanted to work outside.'

'The interview,' says Mum. 'Jakub is terrible at interviews.'

'Not ... terrible,' says Jakub, going all pale. 'I just get ... a little nervous.'

'A little nervous?' Mum replies in that way adults do when they mean the opposite thing. 'At your last interview, you puked all over the manager!'

'You mean he was "A Bit Queasy",' I Helpfully Suggest.

'Your mum's right,' says Jakub, sitting down and shaking a bit. 'There's no way I can do this interview. My stomach's in pieces just thinking about it.'

Oh dear. So Jakub gets worried too. What if he gets Worry Wobbles for his interview? He might set the dragon free ...

'Of course you can do the interview,' says Aunty Amara, taking his hands. 'There are lots of things you can do to help nerves. Let me give you some tips.'

She sits down with Jakub and smiles at him. Aunty Amara is the best.

'Firstly,' she says, 'think about why you are nervous.'

'That's easy,' says Jakub. 'Because I don't want to puke all over Lady Tottington-Snoot.'

'Well, there's that,' smiles Aunty Amara. 'But you're also nervous because you've got a new and exciting opportunity. This is a chance for you to do a job you really love – that's a good thing.'

I think about my nerves about MathsQuest. Actually, that's really exciting too – I've been chosen out of all the kids in my school to represent St Lidwina's. That's pretty cool.

'Secondly,' says Aunty Amara, 'think about what it is that you are worried about. What is it that you think you can't do?'

71

'Well,' says Jakub. 'I've never been a groundskeeper before. I don't have any experience.'

'But Lady Tottington-Snoot obviously thinks you have talent – she's seen what you can do,' says Aunty Amara. 'So she's not looking for your experience – she's looking for your skills, which she already knows you have. She wants to give you this job.'

That's a good point too. Ms Pitt-Bull wouldn't have chosen me for MathsQuest if she didn't think I could do it. If she thinks I'm good enough, perhaps I actually am?

'But when I'm in an interview, no matter how much I plan, I just forget what to say,' says Jakub. 'The words just get stuck in my mouth and my brain freezes.'

Jakub is panting a bit now. He's getting nervous about getting nervous. I start to feel a bit of a Worry Wobble. I'm getting nervous about him getting nervous about getting nervous.

'Breathing is super important,' says Aunty Amara, taking his hand. 'People talk a lot about taking deep breaths, but breathing out is just as important as breathing in. Try this – breathe in for a count of four, then breathe out for a count of six. Do it with me.'

I watch Aunty Amara and Jakub breathe in, so I do it too. I count in 1-2-3-4, then out 1-2-3-4-5-6.

'That's it,' says Aunty Amara, breathing in and out with Jakub. 'The breathing not only helps your body to make sure it's getting enough oxygen, but focusing on the counting stops those gremlins in your head from worrying about what's going to happen, and gives them something else to do.'

'OK,' says Jakub, looking calmer. 'But what if she asks me about lots of different kinds of plants? What if I don't know about them?'

'You know a great deal already,' says Aunty

Amara, pointing to her garden. 'But if there are things you don't know, why don't you spend tonight researching them? Then you can go feeling confident that you have worked on your weaker areas.'

I think about MathsQuest again. I'm really good at multiplication and division, but I'm a bit rubbish at percentages. So that's what I need to practise. This is good advice.

'This is great advice,' says Jakub, looking so much less nervous about being nervous. 'I really do feel better.'

Actually, so do I. I feel the Worry Wobbles die down.

'You'll be fantastic,' says Aunty Amara, giving Jakub a hug. 'I know you will.'

Jakub smiles. We're so lucky to have Aunty Amara. She's always here to give us the best advice ...

Oh.

Except she's not going to be here.

She's going to be in America.

What will we do when we need her advice?

I feel the Worry Wobbles come back. I don't want my aunties to go to America. I want them here with me.

I look at Mum's Easter cake. It's starting to wobble. I try Aunty Amara's breathing ...

In ... 1-2-3-4

Out ... 1-2-3-4-5-6

The Worry Wobbles calm down. The cake stays still. Phew.

'That's it!' Mum suddenly cries, picking up her phone. 'No one is replying to my WhatsApp. They all hate me. I'm going to just ask them outright what I've done to upset them all.'

'Emi, calm down, that's an awful idea,' says Aunty Rosa, trying to take the phone. 'Just sleep on it. They're probably all busy.'

'They all hate me,' Mum cries, nearly hitting her own cake. 'I just know it!'

'It's OK, Emi,' says Jakub, giving her a hug, taking the phone and handing it to Aunty Rosa. 'We all love you. Both of you ...'

He puts his hand on her tummy and I think about the baby coming. I don't want the baby in my polygon. I don't want Polly and Rita in my polygon.

I don't want Aunty Rosa and Aunty Amara to go to America. Why can't Polly and Rita go to America? They can take the snotty, farty baby with them – I want to keep my aunties and my square.

The Worry Wobbles get stronger. I try to breathe, but I forget to count, so I just start panting, which makes me feel dizzy and so I worry about that. Mum is trying to wrestle her phone back from Aunty Rosa right next to the cake, which is wobbling and wobbling closer to the edge of the kitchen counter. Mum is stressed enough without her cake getting spoiled and any second now it's going to go ...

PPPPPPPPPLLLLLLLLLLSPALT!

The big chocolate cake wobbles off the edge of the kitchen counter and splats all over Mum and Aunty Rosa before landing on the floor.

'MY CAKE!' Mum wails. 'It's ... it's ... it's ... TOTALLY RUINED!'

We all look at the Actually Totally Ruined cake on the kitchen floor.

'Maybe you could ask Charlie S to bake you a new one?' Aunty Rosa Helpfully Suggests.

But Mum doesn't find it very Helpful and starts crying about how everything she touches gets TOTALLY RUINED and Jakub and Aunty Amara are trying to calm her down while Aunty Rosa tries to get the phone back from Mum before she calls Rory's mum and it's all getting a bit loud, so I walk out of the kitchen and into the hallway.

I have to get these Worry Wobbles under control. And there's only one person who can help me.

Chapter 2 x 2 + 2

'Darling!' says Granny as she opens her door to me and Maisie after school. 'How lovely to see you! Hello, Maisie, how are you?'

'Very well, Mrs Andrews, thank you for asking. I hope you're well too?' says Maisie, offering her hand.

My granny smiles and shakes Maisie's hand. She likes it when people do things in Polite Olden Days ways and Maisie is *super* polite. She once sent a thank-you letter to Ms Pitt-Bull for a really interesting Geography lesson.

'I'm very well, thank you, Maisie,' smiles Granny. 'But please, call me Nancy.'

Maisie nods her head and smiles.

'Thank you, Mrs Andrews,' she grins. 'I will.'

Maisie and I are having tea at my granny's house today, which is good, because I really need to talk to both of them about my Worry Wobbles. But when I go through to the kitchen, Aunty Rosa and Aunty Amara are sitting at Granny's table with a pile of papers.

'Hey, squidge,' says Aunty Rosa as Aunty Amara gives me a big cuddle. 'Hey, Maisie.'

'Hi, Ms Andrews-Bhatt,' says Maisie, trying to shake hands again.

(That's my aunties' new surname, by the way, because when they got married, apparently they 'double-barrelled' their old surnames. I don't know if they get to keep the barrels, but they're definitely going to keep the name.)

Aunty Rosa laughs and pulls Maisie in for a hug.

'Good to see you, lovely girls,' says Aunty Amara.

'What are you doing?' I ask them, looking at the

table covered in papers.

'To go to America, we need to do lots of paperwork,' Aunty Rosa explains. 'I needed some documents from Mum.'

I pull a face.

'Don't be like that, squidge,' says Aunty Rosa. 'We're going to New York, not the moon. You can come and see us all the time.'

I'm about to tell her that I'm not being like anything, when Aunty Amara interrupts.

'She can be like anything she wants,' she says. 'It's a big change. I'm not surprised she's finding it difficult. We're happy to talk about anything you want to know, baby girl. Just ask.'

And that's why I like Aunty Amara so much. She just understands stuff. Which is why I need her here ...

'Right, you girls – run along for a minute,' says Granny ('*Run Along*' *is Polite Olden Days for* '*Go*

Away', by the way). 'We'll just finish up here and I'll be with you.'

'Let's go and make a playing-card pyramid like we did last time we were here,' says Maisie excitedly. I try to be excited too. Granny only has old-fashioned games like cards and Snakes and Ladders at her house, which are ... Differently Fun. Maisie likes to build pyramids out of cards because she likes games that take a lot of patience. I like them too. I just wish they went a bit quicker.

We sit down in the lounge (*Granny refuses to call it a living room*) and get the playing cards out of the games chest (*Granny refuses to call it a box*). We start to put the cards up in A shapes – you have to do this super carefully or you knock them all down and start again. Once you have a row of those, you have to carefully place another card flat on top and then balance some more As on top. It's really hard. Maisie loves it. I find it very Differently Fun.

'So when are you going to talk to your granny?' Maisie asks, building the last A.

'When my aunties have gone,' I say, balancing a card perfectly on top. 'Granny understands these things. She has **BIG FEELINGS** too.'

'And you're sure it's happening again?' says Maisie, putting a card down next to mine. 'The explosions when you were angry might have been a one-off. After all, you've mostly got them under control now. Well – apart from that time in the canteen ...'

'I'm telling you, it was supposed to be lasagne on Tuesday!' I say, feeling the angry bubbles start to pop at the memory. 'Not boring shepherd's pie!'

'It wasn't very boring when you exploded it all over the canteen,' Maisie points out, and we both laugh, which makes the angry go away.

'But are you sure?' says Maisie, finishing the second row of cards. 'It seems a bit ... unlucky.'

I sit back in my chair and sigh.

'Make me worry about something,' I say to her.

'Pardon?' says Maisie (*Maisie doesn't say What like most people, she's that polite*).

'Go on,' I shrug. 'Then I can prove it to you.'

'Um. OK,' says Maisie, pushing her red glasses up her nose. 'What about ... your new baby brother or sister?'

Oh yeah. The snotty, farty baby. Immediately I feel the Worry Wobbles start in my tummy.

'Keep going,' I say as the wobbles build.

'Er ... and your aunts going to America ...'

The wobbles get stronger.

'And again,' I tell her as my tummy wobbles all about.

'And ... MATHSQUEST!' Maisie shouts (*she's really getting into this now, by the way*).

That's it. That's all I need. The Worry Wobbles fill my tummy and start moving up my body,

making everything wobbly inside. I look at our card
pyramid, which starts to tremble.

'Oh my days!' gasps Maisie. 'Scarlett. You're ...
you're doing it!'

I look at the pyramid and think about babies
and America and percentages. It doesn't take much
– the pyramid isn't very strong, but my worries are.
In seconds, the pyramid collapses with a gentle

FLLLLLLLLLP

Maisie looks at me and looks at the cards on the table.

'NANCY!' she yells at the top of her voice.

'What did you do that for?' I hiss at her.

'Because you need help,' says Maisie as Granny rushes into the room.

'Girls! Are you all right?' she asks, panting a lot, which is weird because she only came from the kitchen.

'We're fine ...' I start to tell her.

'Scarlett's getting her BIG FEELINGS again and this time she's making stuff wobble when she's worried just like she made stuff explode when she was angry,' says Maisie, all in one breath.

'I see,' says Granny, sitting on the sofa to catch her breath. 'Well, it sounds like Scarlett and I had better have a little chat. Maisie – would you mind going into the kitchen and putting the biscuits and cakes on a plate for tea, please? Rosa and Amara can show you where they are.'

'Yes, Mrs Andrews,' says Maisie, giving me a little hug as she walks out of the lounge.

'So,' says Granny, patting the seat next to her.

'So,' I repeat, going to sit on the sofa.

'I can't say I'm terribly surprised,' says Granny. 'The same thing happened to me when I was your age. Every time I pushed down a new Big Feeling, a whole new set of strange things would start to happen.'

'So how did you stop your Big Feelings?' I ask her.

'Why would I want to do that?' huffs Granny. 'You shouldn't stop yourself feeling any more than you should stop yourself breathing. It won't do you any good.'

'But I can't just go around exploding things and making stuff wobble,' I say.

'Well, sometimes you might just find you can't help it,' says Granny. 'Feelings are like that – sometimes they are out of us before we know it. But we can find helpful ways to manage them rather than just pushing them down. Let's get some advice from your Aunty Amara. She's the expert.'

'But she won't be here for much longer,' I sulk. 'Why can't you just stop them from going to America? You're Aunty Rosa's mum. Can't you just ... ground her or something?'

Granny laughs.

'It's not my job to ground my children,' she whispers. 'It's my job to help them fly. Come along,' (*that's Polite Olden Days for 'Hurry Up', by the way*).

'OK,' I grumble. 'But I don't want her to know about this, OK?'

'Your secret is safe with me,' says Granny, tapping her nose. (*I'm not sure if that's Polite Olden Days, by the way, or if Granny just has a really itchy nose.*)

We walk towards the kitchen, which is filled with music and laughter. Aunty Rosa is picking Maisie up to reach one of Granny's high cupboards to get the plates. Maisie is then throwing them to Aunty Amara, who is setting up for tea as she dances around the table. They are having Proper Fun.

'Amara, I wonder if I might trouble you for some advice,' says Granny a bit too loudly. 'I'm finding myself worrying about a few things. I wonder if you might have some techniques that could help me.'

Granny starts winking. Her eyes must be as itchy as her nose. Maybe she has hay fever, like William D (*who sneezed so hard when they cut the football pitch grass last summer, by the way, that he got bogeys in Emma R's French braids*).

'Oh, I see ... Nancy,' smiles Aunty Amara. 'Is anything in particular worrying ... you?'

'I just feel as if a lot of things are changing,' says Granny, really loudly now. 'And it's making me

worried and I don't like it.'

'Understood,' nods Aunty Amara. 'Well, firstly we must remember that worry, like all emotions, is a helpful thing. It tells us if something is slightly off, keeps us safe and makes us think about the consequences of our actions. These are all good things.'

I nod. Then I stop as I realise that this isn't supposed to be anything to do with me.

'I recommended some breathing techniques to Jakub that might help you too, Sc— Nancy,' Aunty Amara continues. 'And often, just taking a minute to use our senses and ground ourselves in the moment can help, by listing five things we can see, four things we can touch, three things we can hear, two things we can smell and one thing we can taste. That can stop your mind from spiralling into worries that aren't in that moment.'

'My mind does that sometimes,' admits Maisie, eating the chocolate biscuit Aunty Rosa has just sneaked off the plate for her. 'Sometimes I worry that I'll never find my Forever Family and I'll have to keep going to lots of different foster families.'

Aunty Rosa takes a very wobbly breath and looks at Aunty Amara, who does a sad smile back.

'Your Forever Family is out there waiting for you, Maisie,' says Aunty Rosa softly, rubbing her eye. 'And they're going to be so lucky to have you.'

Aunty Rosa hugs Maisie and scratches her eye again behind Maisie's back. This hay fever must be *super* catching.

I try Aunty Amara's suggestion, looking around the kitchen at what I can see, touch, hear, smell and taste. It actually helps. And makes me really hungry for the cakes and biscuits.

'But what if using your senses doesn't work, what if I'm ... What if Granny is already worrying?'

'Then sometimes we need to give our brain something else to think about,' says Aunty Amara.

91

'Try making alphabetical lists. The concentration it takes can be enough just to knock our minds in a different direction and let the rest of our body take a moment to calm us down. Let's do it now with animals: aardvark, bear, cat, dog ...'

'Earwig,' says Maisie, which makes Aunty Rosa laugh.

'Ferret,' I add, which makes Maisie laugh.

'G ... green ... fish!' splutters Granny, which makes everyone laugh.

'You see,' beams Aunty Amara. 'Now, I'll tell you something else that makes everyone feel better?'

'What's that?' asks Maisie, giggling as Aunty Rosa tickles her.

'CAKE!' says Aunty Amara, sitting down at the table. 'Come on, everyone. Let's eat!'

We all sit down and have a really fun tea playing the alphabet game.

'You see,' says Maisie. 'Your family always knows what to do.'

She's right. But just as I'm having a really good time, a big Worry Wobble bubbles up in my tummy. Soon I won't have Aunty Amara to talk to. Soon she'll be gone to America. I try to do the alphabet game in my head to stop my Worry Wobbles ...

America

Babies

Competition

Dad and Rita ...

I'll be honest.

It's not helping as much as the cake.

Chapter 14 ÷ 2

Today is the first round of MathsQuest at the Town Hall and I am SUPER nervous. This is where all the schools compete for a place in the semi-final and only one team can go through. There are teams from all the local schools, including our big rivals Holy Trinity CE Primary, who are the first team we are facing today.

Trent has driven us here in the school minibus and he gives us a high-five as we arrive.

'Now, remember two important things,' he says with a grin. 'The first is that at St Lidwina's, we are winners – no, CHAMPIONS! But we're also good sports. You are representing our school, so make sure that you are gracious – no, HUMBLE – when you're winning AND when you're losing.'

Polly and I nod.

'What's the second thing?' Polly asks.

'Don't lose,' says Trent. 'At St Lidwina's, we are CHAMPIONS!'

Trent paces off down a corridor punching the air. Polly and I guess we're supposed to follow behind.

'This is really scary,' says Polly as we walk into a big hall that has been set up like a quiz show, with real buzzers and everything. I can feel the Worry Wobbles starting to build in my tummy. We are taken to our table, where we have some paper and pencils for working out, and a buzzer to hit when we have the right answer.

'I should be in charge of the buzzer,' says Polly. 'You write stuff down.'

'I want to hit the buzzer,' I say, because I really want to hit the buzzer.

'No,' says Polly firmly. 'You do your job and I'll do mine. I'm Team Captain.'

'Says who?!'

'Says me,' says Polly, moving the buzzer closer to her. 'You need to do the writing because—'

'Hey, everyone!' says a man in a silly pointy hat to the audience of two teachers. 'My name is John McHamm! I'm the Mayor of this town – but you probably recognise me from my work with the local amateur dramatic society. I was Dame Anna Chronistic in the last five Christmas pantomimes!'

He looks to the audience. I think he's expecting some applause. He doesn't get any.

'Well ... anyway, welcome to MathsQuest! Now, we want you to remember that everyone here is a winner – except for everyone who loses!'

He laughs. I'm not sure why.

'The rules are simple,' says Mr McHamm. 'I will ask you eleven questions. The team with the most

96

correct answers progresses to the semi-final! The last two teams remaining will go head-to-head in the Grand Final next week!'

'GO, ST LIDWINA'S!! GO, ST LIDWINA'S!!' chants Trent. The other teacher looks at him like he should go on The Cloud for not putting his hand up.

'Come along, HT!' says Mrs Fox, the Head of Holy Trinity, clapping politely. Trent laughs a big spitty laugh. Mrs Fox gives him a Don't Be Like That look.

'Question one,' says Mr McHamm. 'What is the square of nine?'

I know this! I reach over Polly and hit our buzzer.

'Three!' I cry out, looking happily at Trent.

'I'm afraid that is incorrect,' says the Mayor as the Holy Trinity buzzer goes.

'It's eighty-one,' says the boy on their team smugly. 'Three is the square root.'

97

'That is the correct answer!' says Mr McHamm. 'That's one point to Holy Trinity!'

Mrs Fox looks at Trent with a smug smile. Trent says something we can't hear.

'Don't hit the buzzer!' Polly hisses at me.

'I was positive!' I tell her.

'Positively wrong!' she says. 'If you're not sure, don't buzz!'

'But we have to get the points,' I say.

'Will you just—'

'Question two,' says Mr McHamm. 'What is 132 divided by twelve?'

'I know this!' I say, reaching for the buzzer. 'It's eleven.'

'Wait!' says Polly, putting her hand over the button. 'I'm just—'

BUZZ!

The Holy Trinity buzzer buzzes again.

'It's eleven,' says Smuggy.

'Correct!' says Mr McHamm. 'And incidentally, also the number of times I've played Third Villager from the Right in our annual harvest festival play! But that's another point for Holy Trinity!'

'I told you it was eleven!' I snap at Polly.

'You were wrong last time,' Polly grumbles. 'You're rushing.'

'And you're too slow!' I say. 'We need to get a point.'

'Question three,' says Mr McHamm. 'What is six eighths as a percentage?'

Urgh. Percentages. I'm not very good at these. Polly picks up the pencil. I look over at Holy Trinity, who are doing the same.

'OK,' she says. 'First, let's simplify the fraction. What goes into six and eight?'

'Two,' I say quickly. I am so good at multiplying and dividing.

'You're right,' says Polly. 'So if you divide six by

99

two, then eight by two, you get—'

'Three quarters!' I say. 'But what's three quarters as a—'

$$^6/_8 = ? \%$$

$$^6/_8 = {}^3/_4$$

$$^3/_4 = 75\%$$

'Seventy-five per cent' Polly cries, hitting the buzzer. 'The answer is seventy-five per cent!'

'Correct!' says Mr McHamm. 'St Lidwina's are off the mark with one point!'

Polly smiles at me. I'm glad she realises that she wouldn't have got the answer without my help.

But if Polly is pleased, she has nothing on our new head teacher.

'YES!!!' roars Trent, standing up and beating his chest. 'YES! YES! YES! OOOF OOOF OOOF!'

Mrs Fox scowls. Now she says something we can't hear.

Polly and I look at each other. We can do this. Especially if she listens to me and lets me press the buzzer.

The questions keep coming. Polly gets the next one about angles in a triangle right. Holy Trinity get the one after about the number of lines of symmetry in a kite wrong, but I know there's only one. So we get that point too. Holy Trinity get the ratio and units of volume questions right, but Polly knows about prime numbers and I've learned the thirteen times table. But then Holy Trinity win the next point about centimetres in a kilometre (*one hundred thousand by the way*).

'Well now,' laughs Mr McHamm. 'This is more exciting than when I got to understudy Farmer McKenzie in our spring production of *It Shouldn't Happen to a Vet*! Holy Trinity has five points. St Lidwina's has five points. The eleventh question will decide who goes through to the next round!'

'GO, DOTTY! GO, CHARLOTTE!' Trent yells, standing up on his chair and roaring. 'GO FOR THE KILL!'

'COME ALONG, SAMIRA! JOLLY GOOD, KYLE!' shouts Mrs Fox, her hair now a bit messy.

'Question eleven,' says the Mayor dramatically. 'Write down this list: 1, 1, 2, 5, 6.'

I write it out on the paper.

'In this list,' Mr McHamm continues, 'one is the mode, two is the median and five is the range. What is three?'

'Huh?' I whisper to Polly. 'Three isn't even on the list.'

I look over at Holy Trinity. They look confused too.

'It's a trick question,' says Polly. 'What if we add them all up?'

I do it quickly.

'It's fourteen ... No – it's fifteen,' I say. 'How does that help?'

'I don't know,' says Polly, looking panicked. 'Have you got a better idea?'

'Yes,' I say, even though I haven't. 'What if we—?'

'Hurry up,' says Polly as Holy Trinity start scribbling on their paper like they know the answer.

'I'm trying to think!' I tell her, the Worry Wobbles starting in my tummy again.

'Well, think faster!' says Polly.

'You told me to slow down!' I hiss back.

'Well, if you'd got that first question right, we would have won by now.'

'If you'd not stopped me on the second, we would have won more!'

'You're too fast!'

'You're too slow!'

'I'm just better at Maths than you!' Polly hisses.

'That's MEAN!' I say, slamming my hand down on the buzzer by accident just as I say it.

'Yes! MEAN is CORRECT!' shouts Mr McHamm excitedly. 'The total of those numbers is fifteen; if you divide them by five, you get the *mean* of three! St Lidwina's win by six points to five – they progress to the next round! Just like I nearly did on *The Town Council Has Talent* with my stirring rendition of "The Birdie Song".'

'YES! YES! YES!' cries Trent, jumping off his chair and kicking the one in front of him over. 'IN YOUR FACE, HOLY TRINITY! IN YOUR FACE! IN YOUR—'

'Would you mind stepping outside with me,

sir?' says a man in a security guard uniform. I'm guessing he's a security guard. 'We'd just like a quiet word.'

Trent smoothes his hair down and is taken outside. Polly and I can't believe it. We hear tears coming from the Holy Trinity team.

'Please don't cry,' says a soothing voice. 'You tried your very best.'

We watch Smuggy hand Mrs Fox a tissue to dry her eyes. I'm sure she'll feel better soon.

'We did it,' says Polly, looking just as surprised as I am.

'We were lucky,' I say. 'If we're going to win the next round, you need to—'

'Children!' says Mr McHamm, coming over to us. 'Congratulations! Now, there's no official prize for qualifying, but just say the word and I'll get you front-row seats for my one-man comedy show, *Night Mayor*. Bring your family. Mine can't make it for some reason.'

Polly and I look at each other. I wonder what's Granny's Polite Olden Days way of saying 'No Way'?

'Now, you were due to meet St Theresa's RC Primary in the semi-finals, but sadly they've had to withdraw after a positive random test for worms. So you will progress straight to the final, where you will play against Insufficient Prep.'

Insufficient Prep. I recognise that name. Who do I know who goes there?

'Urgh!' comes a horribly familiar voice behind

me. 'I thought I could smell something stinky.'

Oh no.

I turn around. It can't be …

'William U?!' Polly cries. 'What are you doing here?'

'Winning,' says William U. 'I'm the best at Maths in my class. My school's in the final and we're going to beat Stinky Lidwina's.'

'But … but … you were on the Orange Table in Maths!' I say.

'Only at Stinky Lidwina's,' smirks William U. 'At Insufficient Prep, my mum explained that I have Intended Right Answer Syndrome. That means that even if I put the wrong answer on the paper, I know what the right answer is really, so I should still get the mark.'

'That's just made up,' says Polly. 'There's no such thing.'

'Actually, Polly,' says William U's mum, coming

up behind William U and putting her arms around him, 'if you look it up on MyChildCentre.Universe, you'll see it's a brand-new field of research. So let's be nice. Don't Upset My William.'

(*By the way, William U's mum is ... I don't think they've invented a word for her yet. But she invented William U, so her eggs and seeds must have been really rubbish.*)

'I didn't think mums and dads were allowed here today,' I say. My parents and Rita had wanted to come but Trent told them that they couldn't.

'Oh, Scarlett,' laughs William U's mum. 'I'm not here as a parent. I'm here because I've started a new job at Insufficient Prep.'

'You're a teaching assistant again?' Polly asks in surprise (*William U's mum used to be our teaching assistant in Rainbow Class. She was awful, by the way*).

'No, no, no,' says William U's mum. 'I've started a

new role there. I'm Head of External Competitions. It's my job to pick who represents Insufficient Prep when we go to competitions.'

Polly and I look at each other. Of course she is.

'Well – it'll be lovely to see you in the final, girls,' says William U's mum, as William sticks his tongue out at us. 'And just remember, it's the taking part that counts.'

Trent comes over to us with a big grin.

'It's time to go, girls,' he says. 'Well done, you! You were great – no, FANTASTIC! You did St Lidwina's proud. I just wish I could come and cheer you on at the final.'

'Thanks, Trent,' says Polly. 'Why can't you come? Are you busy that day?'

'A head teacher is always busy, Dotty,' says Trent. 'And also – I've just been banned from MathsQuest for life.'

109

Chapter 2 X 2 X 2

Today is the day of Jakub's job interview with Lady Tottington-Snoot. He has been taking all of Aunty Amara's advice and studying and breathing a lot.

It hasn't worked.

'Argh!' he screams over breakfast, running back to his computer for the millionth time (*it's not really a million, by the way, it's more like eight. But Ms Pitt-Bull told me that it's OK to use hyperbole – which means making something sound bigger than it is – when we write for effect, so I'm going to try it out*). 'I can't remember whether you should put manure on shrubs or fruits ...'

'STOP PANICKING!' screams my mum, checking her phone for the two millionth (*actually about sixth*) time as she makes me pancakes. 'I just don't understand – EVERYONE in Rainbow Class says they're busy on the night I want to do the end-of-term drinks. THEY ALL HATE ME!'

'Not as much as Lady Tottington-Snoot is going to hate me when I spread manure on her plums,' says Jakub, frantically searching online (*'manure', by the way, is what gardeners call poo. I don't know whether it's more polite to say 'Number Two' or not, but if you're putting poo all over your garden, you probably don't care all that much about manners*). 'Uh-oh, I need to go again ...'

Jakub runs to the toilet for the one hundred millionth (*maybe fourth*) time. He's making a lot of manure this morning.

Mum puts a big stack of yummy pancakes down in front of me.

'Scarlett,' she says seriously. 'I think you should go with Jakub today, help him to calm his nerves.

He's out of control.'

'OK,' I say.

'What's that?' she says, looking at her phone for the billion and fifteenth (*actually billion and fifteenth*) time.

'I said OK,' I repeat. But she isn't listening.

'Nothing. They hate me,' she whimpers as Jakub comes back in and looks A Bit Queasy at his pancakes. Wow. If Jakub isn't eating his pancakes, he must be nervous. He once ate fifteen WITH syrup.

'I'm going to come with you to your job interview,' I tell him.

'Really?' says Jakub, looking relieved. 'That would be great, thank you!'

He puts a bit of pancake in his mouth. Mum puts a bit in hers.

'Uh-oh,' says Mum, putting a hand to her mouth.

'Uh-oh,' says Jakub, grabbing his tummy.

 112

They both run out of the kitchen.

Thank goodness we have more than one toilet.

As we get close to Tottington Hall, it really does look like a castle. It's a big grey house with turrets and loads of windows. There is plenty of room for a dragon here, so I will make sure I keep my eye out for it.

'Wow – just look at these gardens!' says Jakub as we drive past some hedges that are cut into different shapes. 'This place is amazing.'

I look at Jakub staring around the pretty grounds. I really hope he gets this job. He enjoyed cleaning offices. But this is Jakub's dream (*just like my dream is being an astronaut. Or a horse-rider. Or a chef. Or an Australian. I haven't decided yet*).

We pull up outside Tottington Hall and walk up to the big wooden door. Jakub pulls on the big bell and tries to straighten his tie, but actually makes it wonkier. His hands are shaking, so I hold one and give him a big smile. He tries to smile back, but looks like he needs to make more manure.

The door opens slowly and a man stands in front of us. Granny says it's rude to say people are old and has a Polite Olden Days word for it. So this man is very *distinguished*. And I think he's been distinguished for a really long time. He's wearing a black suit that looks like he's getting married.

'May I help you?' he asks. He's very posh.

'Hi ...' Jakub says, his voice shaking. 'My name is Nowak. I mean Jakub ... I mean Jakub Nowak. I'm here to see Lady Tottington-Snoot.'

'I see,' says the man in the suit, looking Jakub up and down like he's got manure on his clothes. 'To what does this visit pertain?'

(*I have no idea why posh people have to speak in Posh, by the way. They put all their words in the wrong order so it's really hard to understand them. I think he just means 'What are you doing here?' So why not just say it?*)

'It regards to ... I'm pertaining at ... to what I am visiting is,' Jakub gabbles, sweat starting to pour down his head. Jakub really doesn't speak Posh. But I can.

'One is here about the job of gardeningness,' I say in my poshest voice. 'But one must first pertain to the lavatory for to make a Number Two.'

I grin at Jakub. He doesn't grin back.

'I see,' says the man, like he can now smell the invisible manure on Jakub's clothes. 'Please wait in the hall. I shall enquire of Her Ladyship as to her availability.'

(*I think, by the way, that means 'I'll see if she's in' in Posh.*)

Jakub looks nervously around the hall. Our hall has some coat hooks, three years of old wellies and a shelf for the post. Lady Tottington-Snoot's hall has a chandelier, two staircases, a silver tray for her letters and a big piano. I don't know where she keeps her wellies.

'This place,' says Jakub nervously. 'It's incredible.'

'It's very distinguished,' I say, looking at all the cobwebs and dust. Jakub wouldn't let this place get this dirty; he's brilliant at cleaning.

'Her Ladyship will see you now,' says Mr Poshy, leading us down a long corridor to a big brown door. I look out for the dragon.

'You may enter!' comes a posh lady's voice from inside.

Jakub takes a deep breath in for four and out for six. I smile at him.

'You can do this,' I tell him, because I really think he can do this.

He smiles and opens the door.

We walk into a massive room with a glass ceiling and loads of books around the outside. There's another piano in here (*how many pianos do you*

need, by the way?) and in the middle of the room is a ... distinguished lady surrounded by cats. Loads and loads of cats. They all have name tags – there's Stanley and Neville and David and John ...

Lady Tottington-Snoot is wearing a purple dress with a big purple hat and she looks at Jakub through a half-pair of glasses that are on a chain around her neck (*not attached to her head like my glasses are, which seems a bit silly, by the way*) .

'What is that?' Lady Tottington-Snoot says, pointing at me.

'That ... She is my little girl,' says Jakub, putting his arm around me.

'Hi – I'm Scarlett,' I say, waving as a cat called Maggie rubs against my legs.

'Don't. Touch. Anything,' Lady T-S says very firmly. 'My things are very expensive and irreplaceable. Children make a mess. I don't want a mess in my house.'

I feel the Worry Wobbles in my tummy. I wasn't going to touch anything. But now I want to touch everything. But if I touch something and it breaks, Jakub won't get his dream job and it'll be all my fault ...

A vase starts to wobble on the table next to me. I try Aunty Amara's breathing.

In: 1-2-3-4

Out: 1-2-3-4-5-6

The vase stops wobbling. It worked! OK – I can do this.

'I like the look of your potatoes,' says Lady Tottington-Snoot.

'Th-thank you,' stammers Jakub. 'You need plenty of manure.'

I look at Jakub. I don't think this is a good time to tell Lady Tottington-Snoot about his Number Twos.

Jakub goes to smooth his messy hair down – but

he nearly knocks a big pot over, only just catching it in time.

'BE CAREFUL!' Lady T-S shouts. 'That urn holds the ashes of my beloved Winston!'

'I'm so sorry! He was your husband?' Jakub asks, stepping away from the pot.

'Goodness, no!' says Lady T-S. 'He was my cat! My late husband Cyril's ashes are in this box down here under my chair. I think ...'

Ashes?! Cats and husbands get made into ash here?! It must be the dragon ... I'd better be on my best behaviour.

'I see,' says Jakub, looking at the urn and taking another step away.

'He was such a menace,' sighs Lady T-S. 'Always climbing on the furniture. Never did what he was told. Hair dropping everywhere.'

'Winston sounds quite the character,' smiles Jakub.

'Who said anything about Winston?' Lady T-S huffs. 'I was talking about my husband!'

'Oh,' says Jakub, looking like he's shrunk a bit. Careful, Jakub. I don't want you to end up in an urn.

'My last groundskeeper worked for me for forty-two years,' Lady T-S announces. 'He always said he'd work here until the day he died.'

'I'm so sorry for your loss,' says Jakub.

'So am I,' sighs Lady Tottington-Snoot, standing up. 'Firing him was highly inconvenient. But he was just so old. Follow me.'

She walks to the big glass doors at the end of the room and we go outside into the gardens. There's a ginormous (*that's not hyperbole, by the way; it really is massive*) pond in the middle with a fountain and loads of flowerbeds with beautiful flowers everywhere.

'Oh my goodness,' sighs Jakub. 'I'm in heaven.

Look at those hydrangeas! And the roses! And the birds of paradise!'

'You're going to need a lot of manure,' I warn him.

Lady Tottington-Snoot looks at me through her glasses. 'Like the flowers in a garden,' she says, 'children should be seen and not heard.'

I go very quiet. Lady Tottington-Snoot is scary. I don't want to end up in an urn either.

'Now, were you to come and work for me, I'd need you here six days a week,' says Lady T-S, leading us across the garden.

'That's no problem,' says Jakub. 'We live in the town.'

'Oh no,' says Lady T-S, stopping at a spare house she has in her garden. Maybe it's for keeping all her extra pianos. 'That will never do! What if my azaleas need tending to! No – you will come and live here in the accommodation that I provide for you.'

I feel the Worry Wobbles again. Move house? But I don't want to move house. I want to stay in my house! Even with a snotty, farty baby, I want to stay in my house. I love my house. I'll never leave my lovely—

Lady T-S opens the door to the spare house. It's absolutely MASSIVE.

This could work.

'This is where you would live,' she says, her voice echoing around the room. 'It's only got the five bedrooms, but you'd have to make do.'

Five bedrooms? That's one for Mum and Jakub, one for the snotty, farty baby, one for me and two more for me.

Jakub and I step inside. You could fit our whole house inside just the hallway. Even if we put a piano in it.

'This is beautiful,' gasps Jakub. 'Actually, my wife is going to have a baby, so this would be perfect.'

'Well, so long as I don't have to look at it or hear it,' says Lady T-S.

'So children shouldn't be seen or heard?' I ask her, just to check I understand. 'Because that's going to be very difficult.'

Lady Tottington-Snoot looks at me through her half-glasses again. I try not to be seen or heard. I want to go and hide with the dragon.

'Let us go back to the main house,' she says. 'Bertram can make us tea.'

We walk back through the gardens, Jakub shaking with excitement.

'This place is incredible!' he whispers to me. But I'm not so sure. I'm not sure I want to live somewhere where I can't be seen or heard. That's another change. I want my polygon and my aunties – although I could live with having three bedrooms. But why is everything changing so fast?

I can feel Worry Wobbles growing in my tummy.

We walk past the pond and the water starts to ripple. It's happening again ... I try to find five things to look at, but we're walking so fast, it isn't working.

We go back into the glass room and Lady T-S rings a bell before sitting on the sofa. Jakub pats a cushion and goes to sit down too, but Lady T-S suddenly screams.

'STOP!'

Jakub stops, squatting a bit like he's making some more manure.

'What?' he says quietly.

'You are about to sit on Boris!'

Jakub looks through his legs to see who's on the sofa. But there's just the fluffy cushion.

'Boris!' Lady T-S bellows again. Jakub pokes the fluffy cushion, which immediately screeches and leaps off the sofa. It was a fluffy cat.

'I'm ... I'm so sorry,' Jakub stutters, standing up and nearly treading on another cat, Teresa, under his feet. 'I'm just a little bit ...'

The man who talks Posh – I'm guessing this is Bertram – comes in with a load of cakes and sandwiches on little plates stacked on top of each other. The Worry Wobbles go away. Cake *is* good for worries. That's handy. I reach for a big creamy bun and go to eat it.

'Do NOT get any mess on my carpet!' Lady T-S shouts. I freeze with the bun half in my mouth. I don't know what to do. And I can feel the Worry Wobbles starting again. That's it. I don't care about my three bedrooms. I don't want to move to this place where cushions are cats and I have to be seen and not heard and you can't even eat a cream bun. I don't want to leave my nice house, where I can be seen and heard and eat cream buns. I want Jakub to have his dream job, but I don't want to live in this horrid place, where people and cats end up as dragon ashes, I don't want ...

Uh-oh.

The Worry Wobbles are out of control. The little cakes on the plates start to fall off and are immediately jumped on by about fifteen cats (*no hyperbole, by the way*). Jakub and Lady Tottington-Snoot haven't noticed, but I watch the pot of Winston-the-cat-not-Cyril-the-husband's ashes wobble closer and closer to the edge of the table.

'Your working hours will be 8 a.m. to 4 p.m. Monday to Saturday,' Lady T-S continues.

Saturdays? But Jakub takes me to Wet and Wacky at the swimming pool on Saturdays! We love Wet and Wacky; he can't work Saturdays ...

The wobbles get worse. Winston's pot wobbles closer to the edge of the table. I can't push it back on or I'll be seen and heard and maybe turned into ash as well. I try to get Jakub's attention, but I still have the cream bun half in my mouth.

'And you will have one month's holiday to be

taken at a time to suit me. Never in July and August.'

But ... July and August are the school holidays! That's when we go on our camping trips! I don't want Jakub to get this silly job. I just want everything to go back to how it was. I just ...

'And this will be your pay,' she says, handing over a folded piece of paper. Jakub opens it and nearly does a manure on the sofa.

'Wow!' he gasps. I can't see the paper from where I'm sitting, but it must be a lot, like the fifty pounds Aunty Rosa gave me last Christmas. Jakub has a massive grin on his face. He really wants this job. I want Jakub to be happy, but I don't want to lose my house and my Wet and Wacky and my camping trip and my aunties and my voice and my whole body so I can't be seen *or* heard and everything is just changing too fast and the Worry Wobbles are ginormo-massive now (*no hyperbole*) and the big pot of Winston ash is going to fall and I just think

I'm going to ...

'WINSTON!' Lady T-S screams as the pot teeters on the edge of the table and starts to fall. I jump and splat the bun on my face by accident. Jakub jumps up to catch the urn, but he trips over Teresa the cat, falling headlong across the carpet.

'Arrrrrgggggghhhhhh!' he cries as he flies through the air. I close my eyes. I can't watch this. And I have quite a lot of cream on my face.

I hear a thud. That must be Jakub hitting the ground. I wait for the smash as the urn hits it too.

But it doesn't happen.

I open one eye just a bit, so whatever I see won't be as bad.

But it's not so bad at all.

Jakub is lying on the floor. And Winston's urn is lying on him. He stopped it from getting broken.

'Winston!' Lady T-S screams again, jumping up and knocking over the box with Cyril-the-

husband-not-Winston-the-cat's ashes in it, which
Boris quickly Spends a Penny in. She totters over to
Jakub and snatches up the pot.

'You ... you ... you ...' she starts to shout. Jakub is
in so much trouble. And it's all my fault...

'You SAVED WINSTON!'

Wait ... what?

I'm confused.

If Winston's ashes are already in a jar, I think
Jakub's a bit too late to save him.

But Lady Tottington-Snoot is mega-ginormo happy (*or at least smiles for the first time*). She puts Ashy Winston back on the table and helps Jakub up off the floor.

'That's it,' she says. 'I've made up my mind. You're HIRED!'

'Wh-what?' says Jakub.

'The job's yours,' says Lady T-S, putting Winston back on the table and ringing the bell. 'You start Monday. You can move to the house to suit you. Good day.'

Bertram comes and shows us quickly out of the house. We stand in the big driveway as the door closes behind us. I never did see the dragon.

'I GOT THE JOB!' says Jakub, picking me up and dancing around. He is super happy. This is his dream. And I'm happy for him.

But as I think about all the changes to my polygon, I'm not so happy for me.

Chapter 3^2

It's time for me and Dad and Rita and Polly to go to Kamp KwalityTime. My head is so full of snotty, farty babies and dragon ash and moving house and losing aunties and changing polygons that I haven't had a chance to think about Polly's and my plan to split up my dad and Rita. Looking at them in the front seat of the car singing along to olden days songs from the 1990s, this isn't going to be easy.

We pull up outside our 'unique rustic cabin deep in the heart of the forest', which is quite hard to find because it looks exactly the same as the other fifty unique rustic cabins deep in the heart of the same forest. But as I get out the car and look across the lake with all the people doing water sports and hear children running around having fun, I do feel a little spark of excitement. Kamp KwalityTime looks quite fun. Children are allowed to be seen and heard here.

We go inside our cabin and Polly and I run to our room. There's a bunk bed.

'Double bagsie top bunk!' we both say at the same time.

But I said it first.

'Come on, Polly,' Rita says, appearing at the door with Dad. 'You sleep on a high bed at home. Let Scarlett have the top bunk.'

'Scaaaaarlett,' says Dad in the way he always does when he's trying to get me to do something I don't want to do. 'The bottom bunk is so cool! Like sleeping in your own cave.'

I give him a cross look. Why would I want to sleep in a cave? I want to sleep on the top bunk.

'Pollleeeeeeeeey?' Rita says. It must be catching.

'Be kind ...'

'Fine,' says Polly grumpily. 'Scarlett can have the top bunk.'

She throws her bag on the bottom bunk and slumps down on the bed. She's really upset – she must have wanted that top bunk a lot.

Oh well.

I climb up the ladder and put my bag on the bed. It's really awesome up here. I feel a little bit bad that I got it and Polly didn't. But only a tiny little bit.

'We're going to go and ... take a look around,' says Dad, holding Rita's hand. 'Have fun, girls.'

'Take a look at what?' I ask as they shut the door behind them. 'There's two bedrooms and a kitchen – what haven't they seen?'

'You're so immature,' says Polly (*who is the oldest in Rainbow Class, so she thinks that makes her grown up, by the way*). 'They're going next door so they can be alone.'

'To do what?' I ask.

Polly rolls her eyes.

'To kiss, of course,' she whispers.

'Eugh,' I say, unpacking my UniMingo pyjamas and UniMingo teddy.

'Double eugh,' says Polly, unpacking her pyjamas and teddy and throwing them on the floor.

They are exactly the same as mine.

(*Another coincidence, by the way. Polly and I are TOTALLY different. It's just a coincidence how many coincidences there are.*)

'Hey,' says Polly, poking her head through the ladder and looking up at me. 'We need to make a plan. Can I come up?'

'Sure,' I shrug. Making plans can only be better on the top bunk. She climbs up to my bed. On the top. Which is mine.

'So,' says Polly. 'We need to use this weekend

to show your dad and my mum their worst sides. Once they see what the other one is really like, they won't want to go out any more.'

'I know,' I say. 'But how are we—'

'HIIIIIIIIEEEEEEEEEEEE!' comes a high voice and a knock at the door. 'Anybody here for some Kamp KwalityTime?!'

Polly and I look at each other before scrambling down the ladder and out into the living room. Standing in the middle of it is a woman with very blonde hair and very white teeth. She's smiling too much.

'Hey there, Kwality Kampers!' she almost squeals. 'Iiiiiiii'm Becky!'

She points her thumb towards a big name badge that says 'My Name Is Becky' on it, which must really help people who didn't hear her the first time.

'Er ... hi, Becky,' Polly says as Becky lays out a load of pictures on the table.

'Now, you two Krazy Kampers don't want to spend all day in here, do you?' says Becky, putting her hands on her hips and pulling a sad face. 'You want to go and have some Kamp KwalityTime Kapers!'

She spins around and puts her arms up in the air. I hope she's OK.

Dad and Rita come out of their bedroom looking a bit of a mess – they must have fallen asleep.

'Er ... hi,' says Dad. 'Can I help you?'

'No, you can't!' says Becky, putting her hands on her hips and waggling her finger at Dad as if she's cross. I think Becky must have a lot of **BIG FEELINGS** too. 'But I'm here to help you!'

'O ... K,' says Dad. 'Um ... thanks?'

'Yoooooouuuuuuuu're welcome!' says Becky, spinning around on the spot and raising her hands up again. She must be getting dizzy by now. 'So what would you like to do first? Kayaking? Jet-skiing? Rock climbing?'

'Oh, we thought we'd just ... look around,' says Rita, pushing a braid behind her ear.

'WAAAA WAAAA WAAAA!' Becky suddenly shouts, putting her hands around her mouth. I think she's supposed to be an alarm. Either that or she's feeling A Bit Queasy.

'We have a Boring Parent Alert!' Becky shouts like a robot. 'Send Extra Fun! Immediately!'

Rita gives Becky a look that says she might be getting a ride in her ambulance soon. And not in the front seat.

'No, no, no!' squeals Becky. 'We need to get you signed up for some Kamp KwalityTime Kapers! Here I have a selection of some of our most popular extras.'

'Ah,' says Dad, looking like he did when we talked about eggs and seeds. 'We're not planning to do too many extras. This weekend cost quite a—

139

What's included in the price?'

'All the fun you can have,' says Becky, spinning around again.

'Great!' says Dad. 'Well, we'd like to do some swimming and maybe take a boat out on the lake and—'

'WHOA THERE, DADDDY!' Becky screams. 'Your unbeatable package has bought you all the fun you can have ... inside this cabin!'

We all look around the cabin. There's not much room for fun in it.

'But,' says Rita, crossing her arms, 'I thought Kamp KwalityTime was an "all-inclusive adventure".'

'It IS!' squeals Becky. 'Every day is an adventure when you're with the people you love! But I'm here to offer you those extra special experiences!'

Polly and I go and look at the pictures. They do everything here! There's circus skills (£35.99

per person) and horse-riding (*£50 per person*) and someone will even put cucumbers on your face for £40 (*£20 per person after 9 p.m. on Tuesdays*).

'How about this?' says Polly, picking up a picture of a bowling alley (*£32.50 for a family of three, £15 per additional person*). 'We love bowling, don't we, Mum? You love a bit of competition.'

Polly winks at me. I try not to giggle.

'Er ... yes, but we can do that anywhere,' says Rita, shuffling her feet.

'Oh, come on,' says Dad, getting his wallet out of his trousers. 'It'll be fun. Put us down for bowling and ... oooh – the Fireworks Fiesta on the last night.'

Rita gasps.

'I love fireworks,' she says, looking mushily at my dad. 'They're magical.'

'I know,' says my dad shyly. 'It'll be perfect. Although nothing lights up the world like you do.'

141

Oh no. They're going to kiss. They make me want to ...

'BLEUEUEUEUEUEUEURGH!' says Becky, putting her fingers in her mouth. 'Looks like someone's got Pukey Pashing Parents! We'd better get you poor kids out of here!'

'I agree!' says Polly with a grin. 'Scarlett, what would you like to do?'

'Oooh – I want to do the Leap of Faith,' I say, picking up a picture of a platform high up in the trees, with people jumping off it. 'And there's a special deal! It's only twenty-five pounds!'

'Ohhhhhh,' says Becky, pulling a pouty face as she puts some numbers into a calculator. 'I'm afraid that's our Winter Wonderland offer – only bookings on 4 January at 11.45 p.m. qualify. But you can get it for the bargain price of just thirty pounds each!'

'Um, I don't think that's a great idea, kids,' says my dad, who's gone very pale. 'It doesn't look very safe.'

'All of our Kwality Kapers are fully tested to the highest standards,' says Becky, suddenly looking very serious. 'Any accidents are due to the participants not taking adequate safety precautions. The judge was very clear about that. Anything else?'

Polly and I pick a few more pictures each before Dad comes over and tidies them away.

'That's enough, girls!' he sort of laughs. 'Let's leave some time to relax.'

'Of course,' says Becky. 'Perhaps you could try our award-winning spa? It's only a hundred and fifty pounds for a day pass.'

'No.' says Rita firmly. 'I think you've given us quite enough to do. Thank you.'

'Great,' says Becky, handing Dad a card machine. 'Is there anything else I can do for you today?'

'We need more towels,' says Rita, crossing her arms. 'I assume there isn't a charge for those?'

'Of course not!' says Becky. 'Only after the first two.'

'But there are four of us!' Rita argues.

'Kamp KwalityTime cares about our environment,' says Becky seriously. 'So we limit towels to two per cabin. At what cost a greener, cleaner planet?'

'About thirty-seven pounds fifty per person?' I suggest, guessing it would be somewhere between fencing and basket-making.

'Thank you, sir,' says Becky. 'Please can you enter your PIN?'

'Sure,' laughs Dad, smiling at us all as he puts in his number. 'After all, you can't put a price on memories.'

'Of course you can't,' laughs Becky. 'That'll be £342.94.'

ChapTeR a + b
(a = 4 b = 6)

It's been a really busy day. We've done horse-riding (*£75 including riding hats*), canoeing (*£23.50 before 7 a.m.*) , laser tag (*£10 per person with a voucher*), and went to the all-you-can-eat buffet for lunch (*£15 per person, by the way, but I wasn't very hungry so just had a bread roll. And then I got a hot dog (£6.50) an hour later because I was starving*).

But now it's time for the Leap of Faith. Rita is super excited – we're in the hut where they give you your helmet and make you watch a safety video. Dad is very quiet and looks both A Bit Queasy and like he needs a Number Two.

'So are there any questions?' asks Brad, who is

145

our instructor. Brad has big muscles and long hair. He likes climbing, abseiling, snowboarding and teaching families how to do the Leap of Faith at Kamp KwalityTime.

Rita raises her hand.

'How high is the Leap of Faith?' she asks, pointing to the big platform up a high tree, which you have to jump off.

'It's twenty-five metres,' Brad tells us. 'But at the speed you'll be travelling, you'll be back down on the ground in two seconds flat!'

My dad makes A Very Queasy noise.

'Are you OK?' Rita asks him quietly.

'Sure,' says my dad, strapping on his helmet. 'Just ... ate too much at the all-you-can-eat buffet.'

'Well, the climb up there should work it all off nicely!' says Rita, pointing to the high platform.

I look at my dad. I think he might lose his lunch another way.

I start to feel a bit bad. I don't want Dad and Rita to be together. But I don't want my dad to be this scared.

'You don't have to do this if you don't want to,' I say quietly to him.

'No way!' says Rita, slapping him on the back. 'My Bruce is up for anything, aren't you?'

My dad nods weakly. I don't think he's at all up for this particular thing.

We leave the hut and walk over to the big tree we have to climb up to reach the platform. Polly and I start to climb up the ladder and Rita follows on behind. My dad stays on the ground and another little boy climbs up behind us.

'Come on, Bruce!' Rita shouts down.

My dad whispers something that we can't hear.

'What's that?' Rita shouts at him.

'I can't,' says Dad quietly.

'What?' Rita asks again.

147

'I CAN'T!!' my dad screams, taking off his helmet.

'Of course you can!' Rita laughs. 'Come on up here, we'll do it together – look, even this little guy is going to have a go.'

'No!' snaps Dad grumpily. 'I can't do it. Just ... just leave me alone.'

Dad storms off and goes and sits by a tree. Rita looks really surprised. And not in a good way. Polly and I exchange a smile.

'Well, come on girls,' says Rita sadly. 'We'll just have to do this one on our own.'

We climb up and up until we reach Brad at the top of the tree. He clips us on to another rope and smiles at us.

'Welcome to the Leap of Faith!' he says. 'What goes up ... must come down! Who's going first?'

'I will!' says Rita, standing on the edge and jumping straight off. We hear her laugh as she lands

148

on the big net below.

'That was AWESOME!!!' she shouts as she clambers off the net.

'You go, MUM!' says Brad, punching the air. 'Who's next?'

'Do you want to go?' gulps Polly.

'Sure,' I shrug. This is no big deal.

I stand on the platform as Brad clips me on and I look over the edge ...

Suddenly the world starts to go very wobbly. My tummy is like a whirlpool, I can't see straight, I feel A Lot Queasy, I've never been up this high before, it's a gazillion miles down (*no hyperbole*), this is a really big deal and I'm, I'm, I'm ...

'I'M SCARED!!' I scream, holding on to Polly. 'It's too high! I don't want to do it!'

'It's OK,' says Polly. I can feel her shaking too. 'I'm scared as well.'

'If you like, you can jump together,' says Brad,

holding another clip. 'Friends often jump together; it can be very bonding.'

'We're not friends,' Polly and I say at the same time, coincidentally. We both look down at Rita, who is waving happily below.

'Come on, Scarlett,' says Polly. 'We'll be really sad if we don't do it. Think about when TimidMingo didn't want to go to school because he was too frightened.'

'The other UniMingoes helped him to believe in himself,' I remember. 'And they bought him the all-new UniMingo Secret Compartment Pencil Case, which gave him the confidence he needed to do even better at school.'

'Exactly,' says Polly. 'We can be each other's pencil case.'

She holds my hand and smiles at me. That feels really ... nice. I smile back. We nod at Brad.

He clips Polly on and we stand over the edge.

'Now, all you have to do is take a deep breath,' says Polly. 'And we'll jump on the count of three, OK?'

I nod. I think if I say anything all the Queasy will come out.

'You've got this, Scarlett,' says Polly. 'And I've got you. Let's go in one ... two ...'

'Er … Polly,' I tremble. 'I don't think I—'

'THREE!' shouts Polly and jumps up, holding my hand tightly.

'Wait!' I scream as I leave the platform. 'I'm not—'

But it's too late. We are both flying through the air, going down faster, faster, faster until …

DOOF!

We both land in the net.

'Are you OK?' says Polly, laughing and panting all at once.

I look back up at the high platform. I did it! I jumped! It was totally awesome! I feel a different kind of wobbly in my tummy! A good wobbly! Not a worry wobbly! A proud wobbly! An 'I want to do that again' wobbly!

'Yes!' I say to Polly, realising we're still holding hands.

'You GO, GIRLS!' says Rita, punching the air.

She wipes something from her eye. Maybe she has hay fever like William D as well?

'Wanna go again?' Polly grins as we scramble off the net.

Brad explained at the safety briefing that to have another turn, we have to walk around the strictly one-way system, which we're about to do when we hear a big cry. We both look up to the tree. It's the boy who followed us up – he's halfway up the ladder and he's stuck.

'Help!' he cries. 'Help!'

We look back to the tree – we can't get there because there's a big wire fence in the way. A very pregnant lady (*looks like this boy is getting a snotty, farty baby too*) is standing at the bottom of the tree trying to talk him down.

'Just come back this way,' she coaxes. 'One foot at a time. I'm right here.'

'No!' the boy cries. 'I'm going to fall!'

With no one on the platform, Brad has his headphones in (*he likes to listen to dolphins, he told us*) and can't hear. That poor boy, who's going to ... ?

'It's OK,' I hear a trembling voice say. 'I'll go and get him.'

I look at the bottom of the tree. It's my dad. But he can't climb up; he's terrified of heights.

Dad uses his little left arm to grip the ladder and pulls himself up with his right hand. I can see every bit of him shaking, but after a few rungs he calls up to the boy.

'It's OK ... ?' He looks down to the mum.

'Ethan,' she tells him.

'It's OK, Ethan,' says Dad. 'I'm on my way.'

Slowly, shaking with every step, my dad pulls himself up the ladder. At one point he stops and rests his head – it looks like he can hardly breathe.

'Bruce!' Rita cries. 'Bruce, are you OK?'

Dad nods, closes his eyes, takes a deep breath and keeps putting one arm and leg above the other until he gets to where Ethan is clinging on to the ladder, crying his eyes out.

'Hey there,' says my dad so softly I can only just hear him. 'My name's Bruce and I'm really, really scared. Do you think you could help me to get to the top? My little girl's down there (*I wave, by the way, so he knows it's me*) and I really want to make her proud. Will you help me?'

Ethan wipes his eyes and nods at Dad.

'You should always have three touch points on the ladder,' Ethan says, wiping his eyes. 'So either two arms and one foot, or one arm and two feet.'

'That sounds complicated,' says my dad. 'Can you show me?'

Ethan nods and moves his arm and both feet up a rung.

'OK ...' says my dad uncertainly. 'I'm not sure I

got that. Can you show me again?'

Ethan does it again and goes another rung up the ladder. My dad tries to copy him, but can't do it.

'Sorry, Ethan – can you show me that one more time?' Dad asks (*I love my dad, by the way, but he's being a bit silly – he should know how to climb a ladder by now*).

Ethan huffs impatiently and climbs another four rungs up the ladder. Dad follows him up.

'OK!' says Dad. 'I think I'm getting it. But this is really tiring. Can you get up to that platform so I can have a rest?'

Ethan shakes his head and goes up the rest of the ladder, where Brad pulls out his headphones and helps him up. My dad makes it up too. Thank goodness he had Ethan to help him, or he would have been stuck on that ladder all day.

'Nice work, guys!' says Brad, clipping them on.

'Now, what goes up—'

'Oh no. No, no,' says my dad, holding on to the tree. 'I'm fine here, thank you.'

The boy's mum comes up to the net. She's gone the wrong way around the strictly one-way system, but I think they probably just let her.

'Your partner is a hero,' she says to a beaming Rita. 'He's just saved my Ethan.'

Wait ... Dad did what?

I look up at the platform where Dad is clinging on to the tree. Oh ... I get it! He did know how to climb the ladder! He was just trying to get Ethan to climb up himself! Oh, that's really brave! And really clever! And ... really explains how he got me to jump off the diving board at the swimming pool last summer, now I think about it.

'He's a wonderful man,' says Rita proudly.

'He's awesome,' says Polly, looking up at the platform. She smiles. 'You go, Bruce! You're a hero!'

Dad lights up.

'Come on, Dad!' I shout up to my super-brave daddy. 'You can do it!'

'Come on, Bruce,' says Ethan. 'Hurry up – I've got to get to laser tag in ten minutes or my voucher expires.'

My dad nods at Brad, who clips him up.

'Let's go!' says Ethan, jumping off the platform and dragging Dad with him.

'AAAAAAAAARRRRRRGGGGGGGGGG GGHHHHHHHH!' screams my dad as he tumbles down, down, down, until he lands in the net with a big twang.

'Bruce!' Rita cries, scrambling on to the net. 'Bruce! Are you OK?'

My dad lifts his head. He has the biggest grin on his face.

'That was AWESOME!' he yells, punching the air just as Rita reaches him and covers him in kisses.

Bleurgh. They're being all ... fridgey again. 'Let's do it again.'

Polly and I look at each other.

'I don't think that worked,' she says as Dad and Rita skip off together, strictly following the one-way system.

ChapteR 24 – 13

'Is your dad any good?' Polly whispers to me as we enter the bowling alley (*£5.50 supplementary charge for bowling balls*).

I laugh. My dad Finds All Sports a Challenge (*he once scored five goals in the St Lidwina's Parents Friendly Football match – for the Holy Trinity team. Some of his St Lidwina's teammates weren't so friendly after that*).

'No,' I say.

'Good,' Polly grins. 'Then let's put him on a team with Mum.'

'Why?' I ask.

'You'll see,' she giggles, as we head to our lane.

'OK,' says Rita, looking more serious than I've

ever seen her. 'How shall we decide teams? Pick names out of a hat? Rock, paper, scissors? First one to run to that wall over there?'

'Kids versus adults,' Polly says quickly, winking at me.

'Great!' says Bruce, giving Rita a squeeze. 'So good to see you girls playing as a team.'

We smile at each other. If only he knew ...

'Er ... Bruuuce?' Rita asks in a sing-songy way. 'Have you done much bowling?'

My dad spits out his Coke (£3.50).

'You're kidding!' he laughs. 'I'm terrible at it!'

'Uh-huh, OK, yeah.' Rita is smiling, but I think it's one of those pretend ones that people don't really mean. She's clicking her fingers really fast. 'When you say terrible ... ?'

'Unbelievably awful!' my dad says proudly. 'The closest I get to a strike is when my team refuses to play with me any more!'

He laughs. Rita tries to. I don't think she can pretend this time.

'You go first, Mum,' says Polly sweetly, sipping her pink slushie (*£4.25 for two, which is lucky because I dropped my first one*). 'Show us how it's done. You're a pro.'

'Oh well,' says Rita, picking up a ball. 'I wouldn't say that ...'

Rita walks up to the line, holds the ball up to her nose, pulls it back and fires it down the lane ...

CRASH!

The bowling pins fly everywhere as she hits them right in the middle.

'STRIKE!' Rita shouts with a few scary fist-pumps.

'Wow!' says Dad, hitting his hand on his knee. 'You are incredible – that was amazing!'

'It was nothing,' sighs Rita, although she's smiling quite a lot now and I don't think she's pretending.

'Your go, Bruce,' says Polly, chewing on her straw with a smile.

'OK,' grins Dad, picking up his ball. 'Here goes nothing!'

'Oh, come on,' says Rita, sitting down next to me. 'You can't be that bad. He's not that bad, is he, Scarlett?'

I smile and gesture to where Dad has nearly dropped the ball on the floor.

Dad walks up to the line, holds the ball up to his nose, pulls it back ... and lets it go.

Let me explain something:

In bowling there are ten pins. Every turn you get two goes.

If you knock them down with one ball, it's called a strike.

If you knock them down with two balls, it's called a spare.

However many you knock down, that's

your score.

Rita knocked down all the pins on her first try, so she scored ten points, plus whatever she scores with her next two balls.

Dad knocks down ...

... one.

'Yes!' he says, fist-pumping the air. 'I got one!'

'How is that even possible?' Rita says in a strange high voice.

'Don't interrupt me, I'm on a roll,' says Dad proudly, picking up his second ball.

'Maybe if you just aim a bit more ... in the middle ...' Rita Helpfully Suggests. 'And a bit harder. And a bit ... better ...'

'Good idea,' says my dad. 'I'll give this one a real ...'

He pulls his arm back and throws the ball as hard as he can. Unfortunately, he throws it a bit too hard and it flies over our lane and on to the lane

165

next door. It goes straight in the gutter and doesn't hit any pins on either lane.

'Ooooops!' laughs Dad. 'That was a quick roll ...'

He puts his arm round Rita. But Rita isn't smiling, even a pretend one. Rita looks really grumpy.

'You OK?' Dad asks her.

'I'm fine,' Rita snaps back.

'Told you,' whispers Polly, grinning at me.

'Your go.'

I go and pick up my ball. I like to use the special slide to aim my ball, so I line it up, put the ball at the top, then push it down the slide as hard as I can. It goes pretty straight ... and knocks nine pins over! I watch the last one. It wobbles – but it stays up.

'Nice one!' says Polly, giving me a high-five.

'Go, Scarlett!' shouts Dad.

Kamp KwalityTime
Bowling Universe

'Well done,' says Rita politely.

'Looks like we're facing a champion team!' Dad says happily. 'That's why you're going to win the MathsQuest final!'

Urgh. I'd forgotten about MathsQuest. In front of all of those people. In front of stupid William stupid U. What if we mess up again? What if I forget all the answers? What if I'm too fast and Polly's too slow? What if ...

I feel the Worry Wobbles start up. I look over at my dad, who is trying to kiss Rita. What if they get married? What if they have a baby? Then I'll have two snotty, farty babies in both my bedrooms? And I'll be living at Tottington Hall and not be able to be seen or heard, which is going to be very difficult with a snotty, farty baby, and then I'll get turned to cat ash by the dragon and then ...

My head fills up with all the What Ifs and I

can't control the Worry Wobbles. I look at the one remaining bowling pin and it starts to wobble too. It's wobbling and wobbling, just like my tummy and I think it's going to ...

THUD!

With a loud clatter, the one remaining bowling pin falls over.

'YES!' shouts my dad, standing up and punching the air. 'STRIKE!'

'Whoop whoop!' says Polly, as the computer screen starts letting off fireworks.

The Worry Wobbles stop. I got a strike!

Kinda ...

'Nice one, Scarlett,' says Polly, getting her ball and putting it on the slide. 'Now, if I score any more than one, we're in the lead.'

'Er ... no you're not,' says Rita quietly.

'Yes, we are,' says Polly. 'You've got eleven points. We only need two.'

'It doesn't count,' says Rita, not looking at my dad.

'What?' laughs Dad. 'What doesn't count?'

'Scarlett's strike,' says Rita. 'She didn't hit the pin. It fell over. It doesn't count.'

'But it fell over because she hit the others,' smiles my dad, putting a hand on her shoulder. 'It's a strike.'

'No, it's not,' says Rita, shaking him off. 'I'm sorry, Scarlett, but you scored nine. I'll go and see if I can find someone to change the scoreboard.'

'You're not serious?' says Dad. Now he's trying to pretend-laugh. 'You're not really going to get them to take her strike away?'

'The rules are the rules,' says Rita, not looking at me now. 'She didn't score a strike.'

I pretend to look upset – although I'm not really. Rita's completely right. But my dad does look upset. And he's definitely not pretending.

'Rita, they're just kids,' he says. 'Let them have their moment. And besides, it's just a game.'

'Uh-oh,' says Polly, sitting down quietly. 'She's gonna blow ...'

I watch as Rita slowly turns towards my dad. I don't think she's pretending to be upset either.

'It is NOT just a game,' she says. 'It's about fairness and rules and what is right. And we should set the right example to our girls. If you can't respect that ...'

'I can't respect this,' says Dad, puffing up. 'This is daft! It's just bowling! Who cares?'

'So it doesn't matter what I think?' Rita snaps.

'Not when you're being ridiculous,' says Dad. 'This is just ...'

They're fighting! They're actually fighting! We've done it! I turn round to look at Polly – she must be really pleased about this.

But Polly's not there.

As Dad and Rita keep fighting, I look over and see Polly going into the toilets. Dad and Rita are too busy arguing to notice, so I go after her. I just hope that using the Ladies is free here – I haven't got any money with me.

I walk into the toilets and go up to the only closed door.

'Polly?' I ask, knocking on the door. 'Are you OK?'

'I'm fine,' she sniffs.

'No, you're not,' I say. 'You're crying.' (*Because she actually is, by the way.*) 'What's wrong?'

'You won't understand,' says Polly, still crying.

'Well, no. Not if you don't tell me,' I agree.

She doesn't say anything for a minute. But then I hear the door unlock. She's sitting on the toilet lid, holding a soggy tissue to her eyes. I pull some clean tissue from the roll.

'Here you go,' I say.

'Thanks,' she says, giving me the soggy one. It's really gross, but I don't want to make her cry any more, so I just put it in my pocket.

'Your plan worked,' I tell her. 'They're fighting out there. Your mum REALLY likes to win!'

'You have no idea,' says Polly, wiping her eyes. 'She was banned from my last school's sports day for trying to get another mum disqualified from the egg and spoon race.'

'Wow,' I say, handing her some new tissue. 'So why are you crying?'

Polly takes some wobbly breaths.

'It's ... it's my dad,' she says. 'Seeing Mum and Bruce fight reminded me of our family bowling trips. We used to go a lot and he and my mum would always get into a really big fight.'

'Ah,' I say. 'That must have been nice.' (*I'm not really sure what I'm supposed to say to that.*)

'It was horrible,' laughs Polly. 'They'd get in a

really big fight, then someone would storm off and one of them would go home in the car and one on the bus.'

I nod. When my mum and dad were still married, they used to fight a lot. I remember going home in separate cars and buses too.

'That's rubbish,' I say.

'It was,' says Polly. 'But that's the thing. At the time, I just wanted everything to be happy. But now I wouldn't care if we were happy or scared or

angry or sad. I just want my daddy back.'

She starts crying. A lot. I hand her some more tissue, but I know that's not enough to make her feel happy. What can I do to help? How can I make Polly feel better? What will make her smile again?

An idea floats into my head.

'Polly,' I say softly, putting my hand on her knee. 'Would you ... would you like the top bunk tonight?'

Polly looks up with big wet eyes. She smiles.

'Yes, please,' she says. 'I really would.'

'OK,' I say, because I mostly mean it.

We stay there for a while until her tears run out. I tell her about the time my mum and dad had a fight over who sat where on a ghost train and she laughs. She tells me about the time her mum and dad had a fight over which fish to buy in the supermarket and I laugh. And when she's feeling better, we go back out to our lane.

But Dad and Rita aren't there.

'Girls!' we hear from a few lanes away. 'We've moved!'

We go to our new lane, which has big bumpers in the gutters, so no balls can go in them.

'Voila!' says Dad, holding a grinning Rita. 'Bumper Lane! And it only cost five pounds per person more!'

'Polly?' says Rita, looking concerned at Polly's puffy pink eyes. 'Are you OK?'

'I'm fine,' says Polly, looking at me. 'Scarlett looked after me.'

Rita gives me a big smile. It's not a pretend one.

'That's really kind of you, Scarlett,' she says, giving Polly a big cuddle. 'And I truly apologise for being silly. I get ever such a teeny tiny bit competitive sometimes.' (*I think that's hyperbole, by the way.*) 'Would it be OK if I gave you a hug to say sorry?'

I nod my head and she gives me a big hug. It feels really nice.

'Can we be friends again?' Rita asks.

'Yes, we can,' I smile.

And weirdly, I'm not pretending either.

Chapter (3 x 3) + 3

'We're just going to have to accept it,' sighs Polly in bed the next morning. 'We're never going to split them up.'

'I know,' I say, lying next to her. I went up to the top bunk so we could whisper together and have a midnight feast and our parents wouldn't hear us and I must have fallen asleep up here. Dad and Rita have now gone on a Romantic Boat Ride on the Lake (*£34 for 20 mins*) and we're still in our pyjamas in bed.

It's true. We've tried everything. We sent them fencing – but Rita and Dad just ended up tickling each other with their swords. We thought rock-climbing might work, but my dad is now so into heights, he and Rita started to plan a holiday to Mount Snowdon. At dinner we played card games, but the grown-ups just got so tired they had to go to bed early. This holiday has been a total failure.

'They're a couple,' says Polly. 'We're just going to have to get used to it.'

'I guess so,' I agree, cuddling Polly's UniMingo (*we agreed swapsies in the night so we could cuddle both our UniMingoes, by the way*). It's weird – I should feel worse about this than I do. Maybe I'm just tired from all the Kapers.

'But,' Polly starts, 'I've been thinking. Maybe it's not ... like ... the worst thing ever. Them being together, I mean.'

'Me too!' I say, a little more loudly than it sounded in my head. 'I mean ... we can both share our UniMingo stuff ...'

'And go on more weekends like this ...' says Polly.

'Perhaps we could get bunk beds in my

179

bedroom!' I say.

'Bagsie top bunk!' we both say at the same time, and laugh at the coincidence.

'Well, maybe I could get bunk beds at my house too!' Polly says, sitting up. 'Then I could have top bunk at my house and you could have top bunk at your house!'

'And we could cuddle each other's UniMingoes when we have sleepovers,' I suggest.

'And we could share clothes and hair bands and stuff!' Polly says.

'YES!' I shout (*Polly has the BEST clothes and hair bands and stuff, by the way*).

'And we can watch *UniMingoes 2: The Search for UniMingoLand* when it comes out!' Polly says.

'And then we could actually go to the actual UniMingoLand when it coincidentally opens that same week!' I say. 'And then we could—'

There's a knock on the door.

'Girls?' I hear Dad say on the other side of the door. 'Can we come in?'

'Sure,' says Polly, kissing my UniMingo before handing to me, and I kiss and hand over hers.

Dad and Rita walk slowly into the room. Rita is wearing sunglasses, so I can't see her eyes. But I can see Dad's. They're pink and puffy. I didn't know he had hay fever like William D. I hope he didn't get bogeys in Rita's hair.

Dad and Rita sit down on the sofa in our room. They're not holding hands. Or kissing. Or giggling. That's unusual.

'Polly ... Scarlett,' Rita begins. She sounds like she has a sore throat. She can probably fix that in her ambulance. 'We want to talk to you. We know what you've been doing this weekend.'

Polly and I look at each other.

'What do you mean?' I ask, the Worry Wobbles starting up in my tummy.

181

'We know you've been trying to split us up,' says Dad.

Uh-oh.

Busted.

'We're not angry,' says Dad (*who also has a sore throat, by the way. He must have caught it off Rita after all that kissing*). 'We understand. You don't want us to be together.'

'Well ... not exactly,' I say, looking at Polly.

'It's ... complicated,' says Polly, looking at me.

'You don't have to explain, we get it,' says Rita. 'We've been so excited, we haven't stopped to think about how this might be affecting you two. And we're sorry.'

Polly and I don't know what to say. So we say nothing.

'You've both been through a lot of changes,' says Dad, his words getting a bit croaky. 'And we understand that maybe this is one change too many. So ... so ...'

Dad gets up and starts clearing his throat. Rita wipes something from behind her sunglasses.

'So we've decided,' she says, 'that it would be

better if we … If we went our separate ways.'

Polly and I look at each other again. That is Posh or Polite Olden Days talk. But I don't need anyone to translate it.

Dad and Rita are breaking up.

'You … you don't have to do that,' I say.

'No – we want you to be happy,' says Polly, looking very unhappy.

'That's very generous of you, girls,' says Rita. 'But we're not stupid. We know that you two aren't exactly the best of friends. And it's not fair of us to force you to be.'

I look at Polly sitting in the same pyjamas with the same teddy in the same bed. Rita's got a point. It's a shame we don't have more in common.

'Well … are you still going to be friends?' Polly asks quietly.

Dad and Rita look at each other.

'One day,' says Dad with his croaky voice. 'But

184

for now, we think it's best if we take a bit of time away from one another. Just until we're ... feeling a bit brighter.'

I look at my dad, I look at Rita and I look at Polly.

I did it.

I got Polly out of my polygon.

So why don't I feel better about it?

'So pack up your things. We're heading home,' Rita says to Polly.

'But ... but what about the Fireworks Fiesta tonight?' I say. 'You were both really looking forward to it? You said it was magical? You said it was perfect? You said it was £46.99?'

'Another time, love,' says Dad, wiping his soggy eyes. 'We're not really in the mood today.'

'Come on, Polly,' sniffs Rita. 'Let's get going.'

Polly looks at me with sad eyes. She climbs down out of the top bunk and gets her rucksack.

'Wait a minute,' she says. 'How are we all getting home? We all came in Bruce's car.'

'We're going to get the bus home, baby,' says Rita.

'Oh,' says Polly. 'OK then.'

I get down and start to pack my bag too.

I feel A Lot Queasy.

We're going home.

We're going home in separate cars and buses.

'Hey, pickle!' says Jakub at my front door. 'How was Kamp KwalityTime?'

'It was ... fine,' I tell him, looking at my dad's sad face.

'Oh. I see,' says Jakub, looking at Dad as well. 'Bruce, do you want to come in for dinner? Emi's making spaghetti bolognese. She's actually cooked the meat and everything.'

'No thanks, J,' says my dad, accepting Jakub's

186

hug before turning away quickly. 'I ... er ... I need to get home. See you, sweetie.'

Oh no.

Sweetie.

Things must be bad.

He hurries back to his car without giving me his tickly beard kisses. I watch him get inside, wipe his eyes and drive away.

'Come on, monkey,' says Jakub, putting his arm around me. 'Let's see how much spaghetti we can suck in in one breath.'

Jakub picks me up and shuts the front door. Everything's back to normal. I've got my square back.

But then I remember that when I'm not there, my dad doesn't have anyone to make a polygon with.

He's just a straight line.

All on his own.

Chapter 14 + 12 - 13

This afternoon, St Lidwina's Primary School is going to attempt to break the world record for stacking sugar cubes. All our homework has been sugar-cube stacking, we've had special sugar-cube-stacking training sessions, we've been stacking sugar cubes all week and even had an assembly from a man who stacked sugar cubes back in 1974. Today is the day Trent is due to put the WORLD-BEATING sugar cube on top of the tower.

'I never thought I'd say this,' says Maisie. 'But I never want to see sugar ever again.'

I agree. It turns out that stacking sugar cubes is really boring.

It's the end of the day and we're all in the hall. I

see Mum, Granny and Jakub come in and I go over to see them.

'I can't look any Rainbow Class parents in the eye!' wails Mum. 'They all hate me!'

'No they don't,' says Jakub. 'But why don't you just ask someone what's going on?'

'I can't do that!' Mum whimpers.

'Why ever not?' huffs Granny, wiping her forehead.

'Because it will TOTALLY RUIN all my friendships!' says Mum.

'With all the people you think hate you?' Jakub asks.

'Who told you that?' Mum cries. 'So it's true!'

(*By the way, Jakub has explained to me that the reason Mum is acting a bit weird is because the baby makes her have hormones. These hormones can make her sad, stressed, tired and ... a bit weird. I don't know exactly how it works, but if I had a snotty, farty baby in my tummy, I'd probably act a bit weird too.*)

'Scarlett darling, do you think you can find Granny a chair?' Granny asks. 'My old legs are a bit shaky today.'

'Sure,' I say. She looks really pale and not quite as formidable as usual.

I'm walking over to the chair cupboard when I run into Dad.

'Hey, squidge,' he says quietly. I love my dad, but he looks really rubbish. His tickly beard is all straggly and he has big bags under his eyes (*this is what you call those dark circles adults get when they're tired, by the way. He's not really holding actual bags under his eyes*). He still looks really sad. 'What are you doing?'

'I'm just getting a chair for Granny because she's got shaky legs,' I say, trying to pick one up off the high stack.

'Here – let me get that for you, I'll take it

over to—'

'Hey, Bruce.'

Dad drops the chair and spins around. Rita is standing behind him.

'Oh ... hey, Rita,' he says, running his hand through his messy hair. 'How are you?'

'Great,' she says, looking completely ungreat. 'Really great.'

'Great,' says Dad.

'Great,' says Rita.

They don't say anything else. I think they've run out of Greats.

'Well ... I'd better deliver this chair,' says Dad.

'Oh – sure,' says Rita. 'See you ... I mean, take care.'

'You too,' says Dad, with big, sad eyes.

They stand there and look at each other for a moment, before Rita walks over to one side of the room and Dad goes over to Granny. Polly comes up to me.

'Hey,' she says.

'Hey,' I say back.

'How's your dad?' she asks.

'A bit pants,' I say. 'He's really sad and he smells.'

'My mum is a mess,' says Polly. 'All she's done is eat ice cream and listen to sad love songs from the 1990s. It's tragic.'

'Do you ... do you think we did the right thing?' I ask, the Worry Wobbles starting in my tummy.

'Sure,' says Polly, not sounding very sure. 'They'll get over it. Adults just need a bit of time to adjust.'

'Sure,' I say, not sounding very sure either.

Maisie comes running over.

'Scarlett, Polly – come on!' she says. 'Trent is about to put the last sugar cube on top of the tower!'

We go to the front of the hall, where Trent is standing on top of a big ladder. I think about Dad and Rita. I didn't want things to change, but

I didn't want to make my dad really sad. It's bad enough with Mum's hormones spilling all over the place and a snotty, farty baby coming to a house where I have to be seen and not heard. Aunty Rosa and Aunty Amara are leaving for New York next week and it's the MathsQuest final tomorrow and instead of revising my times tables this week, I've been stacking sugar cubes in every lesson, so I don't feel very ready at all.

'Scarlett?' Maisie whispers. 'Are you OK? Is it the ... ?'

I nod my head and do my breathing. I'm trying to control my Worry Wobbles.

'Guys!' says Trent standing in front of the sugar-cube tower. 'If I could just have your attention!'

Everyone goes quiet.

'As you know, here at St Lidwina's we are champions – no, WORLD BEATERS!' Trent roars, punching his arm dangerously close to the tower and making everyone gasp. 'We believe in pushing ourselves [*punch, gasp*], we believe in smashing challenges [*punch, gasp*] and we believe in blasting down every obstacle in our way [*big punch, big gasp*].'

Ms Pitt-Bull whispers something in Trent's ear and he steps away from the tower to climb up the ladder.

'This!' he cries, pulling a sugar cube out of his pocket, 'is the world-beating sugar cube. I'm going to place it on the top of our sugar-cube tower – no, sugar-cube MOUNTAIN!'

But I can only just hear Trent over my Worry Wobbles. (*Breathe in 1-2-3 ...*) What if Dad is all on his own for ever because I broke him and Rita up? (*Breathe out 4-5-6 ...*) What if he's lonely and sad just because I didn't want to change my polygon? (*Am I breathing in or breathing out now, I can't remember 7-8-9 ...*) What if he hates me for making him lonely and sad? (*No idea what I'm doing now 13-25-64 ...*) Perhaps Lady Tottington-Snoot is right and I should be seen and not heard and turned into cat ash if all I'm going to do is make people lonely and sad and ...

Uh-oh.

The Worry Wobbles are getting out of control. I try to breathe, but all I can think about is my dad being lonely and sad and me in a house where the only things I can see and hear are a snotty, farty baby and everyone laughing at me when I get all the answers wrong in MathsQuest tomorrow and no aunties to help and ...

I try to focus on the sugar tower, where Trent is making another speech and waving his arms around. The tower is teetering and everyone gasps again. I close my eyes. Everything is just so scary and confusing and that tower looks really wobbly now and I don't know what to do and I close my eyes because I have a really horrible feeling that if I can't stop this, then our world-beating sugar-cube tower is going to ...

CRAAAAAAAAAAAAAAAAASH!

(*By the way, I don't know if you've ever heard 2,669 sugar cubes falling to the floor. But it's quite loud.*)

At first no one knows what to say. The whole room just stands there in shock.

But then one person starts laughing. Then another person starts laughing. And then all the people next to them laugh, then more than half of everyone is laughing and suddenly the whole hall is full of laughing. All the adults are laughing so hard that some of them are actually crying or bending over or taking pictures on their phones.

Except for Trent, that is, who doesn't seem to find it very funny at all.

'THIS ISN'T HOW WINNERS BEHAVE!'

he shouts. 'YOU
WON'T BE
LAUGHING WHEN
HOLY TRINITY
CE PRIMARY SETS
THEIR WORLD
RECORD FOR
PICKING UP
SWEETCORN WITH
A COCKTAIL STICK!!
NOR WHEN YOU'VE
FOUND OUT I
SPENT ALL OF
NEXT TERM'S BUDGET FOR PENCILS ON
SUGAR CUBES!'

But everyone is laughing too hard to hear him –
even Mum as I walk back over to my family.

'Oh my,' she says, wiping a tear from her eye.
'That was hilarious.'

A group of Rainbow Class parents come over, looking really serious. Mum stops laughing.

'Emi,' Emma R's mum says very seriously. 'We need to talk to you.'

'Oh,' says Mum, looking worried. 'What about?'

'It's about your WhatsApp post about a night out,' says Vashti's dad. 'I'm afraid none of us want to do it.'

'I knew it,' says Mum, starting to get hormoney. 'Why not? What have I done?'

'Because ...' says William D's dad, pulling a big card out from behind his back. 'We want to throw you ... A BABY SHOWER!!! Congratulations on your pregnancy!'

Everyone starts clapping and pulling party poppers and hugging my mum and Jakub. Awwww. That's really nice.

'Oh ... oh ... oh,' smiles Mum. 'You are the best! I'm so happy! I'm just so very ...'

And she starts crying her eyes out.

'So we're going to all get together next Tuesday, as you suggested,' says Emma R's mum. 'And do you know what I thought might be a good idea?'

'What?' smiles my mum.

'If everyone could make Helpful Suggestions on the WhatsApp group!'

Uh-oh ...

But Mum looks really happy now. All that worrying, and everything was OK. Silly Mum.

Now, if only I knew all my own worries were going to be OK. I'm still really worried about—

'Scarlett, dear,' says Granny from her chair. She looks really, really unformidable now. 'Can you fetch me a glass of ...'

Suddenly Granny's eyes go all funny. She wobbles around in her chair.

'Granny!' I cry. 'Granny!'

'OK, Nancy,' says Jakub, running over and

catching Granny before she falls on the floor. 'I've got you. Could someone please call an ambulance.'

'Mum!' my mum cries, kneeling down on the floor where Jakub is lying Granny down. She's gone to sleep. Why has my granny gone to sleep? It's only four o'clock and she doesn't normally fall asleep unless it's ten o'clock and the telly's on. Why won't my granny wake up? What's wrong ... ?

Suddenly there is a blur of someone racing across the room.

It's Rita.

'OK, if you could just clear some space,' says Rita, rushing over and kneeling down next to my granny. 'Nancy! Nancy, can you hear me?'

I can't move or say anything. I feel Maisie come and take one of my hands and Polly take the other.

'Don't worry,' Polly whispers. 'My mum's really good at this. She'll look after your granny, I promise.'

I look at my granny lying asleep on the floor. Why won't she wake up?

'She's breathing,' says Rita to my mum, putting her head on Granny's chest while holding her wrist. 'Nancy! Can you hear me? Nancy, it's OK, you're safe. I'm just going to check a few things and the ambulance is on its way. We've got you.'

I watch as Rita does lots of little tests on Granny.

She's really good, even without her ambulance. She tells everyone what's going on and she makes us all feel much calmer. But Granny still won't wake up.

'It's OK,' Maisie smiles at me. 'She's going to be OK, I just know it.'

I nod. I'm not so sure. But after what feels like five thousand hours (*not hyperbole*), Granny moves her head.

'Emi?' she mumbles. 'Emi, where are you?'

'I'm here, Mum,' says my mum, looking super relieved. 'We're all here. The ambulance just arrived.'

'Oh, poppycock,' (*that's a Polite Olden Days way of saying something really rude, by the way*) says Granny fuzzily, trying to get up. 'I don't need an ambulance.'

'Nancy,' says Rita firmly. 'You need to stay still. My colleagues are going to take you to hospital. You need to get this properly checked out. Just lie down. We're going to help you. But *you* need to help you too.'

My granny quietly puts her head down on the jumper Jakub has put underneath her.

Wow.

Rita just out-formidabled my granny.

A man and a woman in green overalls come into the hall. They are paramedics, like Rita.

'Hi, Priya. Hi, Sam,' says Rita. 'This is Nancy Andrews, seventy-eight, history of Cadillac, a vest and hippo tension. Pulse a hundred and ten, no sign of Hen Ridge.'

(*I think that's what she's saying, by the way, there are quite a lot of long words that I don't understand.*)

'Thanks, Reets,' smiles Priya. 'Good to meet you, Nancy. Sam and I are going to give you a lift to the hospital so the doctors can look you over. We'll even smack the blue light on so we can get home for our tea faster.'

'What utter rot,' grumbles Granny. 'There's nothing wrong with me, I just nodded off for a second.'

'Mum!' says my mum, looking really upset. 'Just do as you're told!'

Wow. I've never seen my mum tell her mum off before. I didn't know you could tell your own mum off.

I might have to try it.

The paramedics lift Granny up on to a trolley (*an ambulance trolley, not one like the ones you get at the supermarket, by the way*) and wheel her outside.

'You go with her,' says Jakub to Mum. 'I'll take Scarlett home.'

'But what about the car?' Mum asks.

'You both go,' says Dad, putting his arm round me. 'I'll look after Scarlett tonight. You should be with Nancy. We'll be fine, won't we, squidge?'

He smiles at me and I try to smile back. I'm

really worried about my granny. But I've never been happier to have my square around me.

My mum goes to leave, but before she does, she sees Rita. She runs to her and hugs her.

'Thank you,' she says tearfully. 'You were wonderful.'

'Just doing my job,' says Rita, as Jakub gives her a hug too and then they both hurry out. Polly and Maisie both put their arms around me.

My dad comes over and hugs us all.

'Come on, you,' he says, giving me a big squeeze. 'If this isn't a night for takeaway pizza, I don't know what is.'

Maisie and Polly give me hugs and Dad takes me outside as the other parents start to pick up the 2,669 sugar cubes. We pass Rita, and Dad stops right next to her. He smiles sadly at her.

'She's right, you know.'

'Who is?' asks Rita.

207

'Emi,' whispers Dad. 'You are wonderful, Rita. Really, really wonderful.'

He puts his arm round my shoulders and walks me out to the car.

Dad's right. Rita is wonderful. She saved my granny today.

Now I need to save my dad and Rita.

chapter 100 - 86

'It's all utter balderdash!' says my granny, sitting up in her hospital bed the next morning (*'Balderdash' is a Polite Olden Days way of saying ... Actually, I have no idea about that one*). 'I'm absolutely fine.'

'You're not fine, Mum,' says my mum, telling her mum off again. (*I tried telling my mum off this morning. It doesn't work, by the way.*) 'You need this operation.'

'I've told you. I am NOT having a silly operation.'

'MUM!' shouts Mum, looking really cross and scared at the same time. 'You heard what the doctor said.'

'That doctor was twelve years old,' huffs Granny.

'That doctor is a senior cardiac consultant! If

209

you don't have this operation, you could ... Rosa, tell her!'

Mum looks at Aunty Rosa, who is unusually quiet and very pale.

'It's for the best, Mum,' says Aunty Rosa. 'You need to listen to your doctors.'

I feel the start of a Worry Wobble. I don't want Granny to ... whatever Mum was about to say. I want her to get better and come home.

'We'll take care of you, Mum,' says my mum. 'Rosa and I. They said you'll need to be here for a few days after the op, but then you can come and recover at Rosa's house. She's got plenty of space, and I'll come over and—'

Mum stops as she realises that Granny can't go to Aunty Rosa's house. Because Aunty Rosa won't be there. She'll be in America. Looking at Aunty Rosa's face, I think she knows it too.

'I'll do everything I can to help,' says Aunty Rosa

very quietly. 'Perhaps I can pay for a nurse to help you.'

'You'll do no such thing,' says Granny formidably, arranging her sheets. 'I *don't* need a nurse – because I *don't* need an operation.'

'But, Mum ...' my mum pleads.

'Enough!' says Granny. 'I'm not having it and that's final!'

Mum and Aunty Rosa give each other a worried look. And that makes the Worry Wobbles worse. If Granny doesn't have this operation, she could ... she could ...

I look at Granny's cup of tea as one of the Five Things I Can See ... but the other four are all nurses and doctors and machines and my poorly granny, and now the cup is starting to wobble and I don't know what I'm going to do if something happens to my granny and ...

'Like I said,' Granny says, looking at me sideways.

211

'I know what's best for me. And right now what's best for me is a cup of tea. A PROPER cup of tea – not that old dishwater they tried to give me this morning. And a nice piece of chocolate cake. Please can you two go to the cafeteria downstairs and get them?'

(*'Cafeteria' is a Polite Olden Days way of saying cafe, by the way.*)

'OK,' sighs Mum, getting out her purse. 'Scarlett, come with me.'

'No,' says Granny firmly. 'Scarlett can stay here with me. You two go.'

Mum and Aunty Rosa don't look very happy about it, but they do leave for the cafeteria. I guess you always have to do what your mum tells you, even when you're a grown-up.

That's a shame.

Granny looks at me funny and gestures for me to come and sit on her bed.

'Now then, young lady,' she says. 'What's going on?'

'You fell over,' I remind her. Maybe she hit her head if she can't remember.

'I mean – with that,' she says gently, looking at the cup of tea, which has stopped wobbling now.

There's no point in lying to my granny, so I tell her all about how I'm really worried about her being poorly and the baby coming and Dad and

213

Rita splitting up and us all moving to Tottington Hall and Aunty Rosa and Aunty Amara going to America. I talk about the Worry Wobbles and the chicken and the eggs and the cake and the sugar cubes and how I don't want to do MathsQuest this afternoon because I'm too scared.

'Well, I don't want to have this silly operation this afternoon,' whispers my granny. 'Because I'm a bit scared too.'

'You are?' I ask her. 'I didn't think you were scared of anything. Except mobile phones.'

Granny laughs.

'Oh, I'm scared of lots of things,' she says. 'I get Worry Wobbles too.'

'So how do you control them?' I ask.

'Well,' sighs Granny, 'there's no one right way. Worries are different, so the solutions are different. Some things you're worrying about, you don't need to worry about. Look at the state your mother got herself into over that silly PlopChat group – and they were just trying to do something nice for her!'

I laugh. Granny really is scared of phones.

'Then there are worries that you need to let other people worry about,' she says. 'Like your father and Rita. That's for them to sort out, not you. They need to make up their own minds about what they're going to do. Just like Aunty Rosa and Aunty Amara going to America. Those worries are very hard to deal with because they are out of your hands.'

'So what makes those better?' I ask.

'Time,' smiles Granny. 'They just take time. And then there's the kinds of worries that you are facing today. Things that we don't want to do. But we have to do them.'

'Like your operation?' I say.

'I ... er ... well ... that's a bit different,' Granny says, sounding less formidable than usual. 'You can't let your school down. They're relying on you.'

I hold Granny's hand. I don't understand.

'But that's not different!' I tell her. 'You can't let me down! I rely on you!'

Granny looks at me, but doesn't say anything.

'I was so scared yesterday,' I tell her, 'when you fell over.'

'I know you were, darling,' says Granny softly, squeezing my hand. 'And I don't ever want you to be scared like that again. But I do want you to do something for me.'

'What?' I ask her.

'Go out there and give that MathsQuest your best shot today,' says Granny, giving me a gentle punch on the arm.

'But ... but I'm really scared,' I tell her.

'So am I,' whispers Granny. 'But think how much better you'll feel tomorrow.'

'What if I mess it up?' I say. 'What if I get all the

216

answers wrong? What if I fail?'

'Then the world will keep on turning,' says Granny. 'But at least you tried. You won't fail if you lose. But you can't win if you don't go.'

'I don't know ...'

'I'll tell you what – we'll make a deal,' she says with a deep breath. 'If you go and do MathsQuest, I'll ... I'll have this silly operation.'

'Really?' I say.

'Really,' says Granny.

I don't have to think about this for very long. I really want my granny to have her operation. I have to do MathsQuest.

'OK,' I say, standing up. 'I'll do it.'

'Me too,' says Granny, as Mum and Aunty Rosa come back with her cup of tea and cake. 'Then that's settled.'

'Here you go,' says Mum, putting them down on Granny's table. 'Tea and cake.'

'Oh – silly me,' says Granny, settling back down on to her bed. 'I quite forgot – I'm not allowed to eat or drink anything before this operation. And you need to go if you're going to drop Scarlett at MathsQuest.'

'But I thought you weren't ... you said ...' says Aunty Rosa, looking all confused.

'Oh, do try to keep up, girls,' says Granny formidably. 'Emi, you're taking Scarlett to MathsQuest. Rosa, you can stay here with me until Emi gets back and then I'll have this blasted operation and we'll all be done by teatime. Now, run along – and as for you, Scarlett – you can have this nice piece of chocolate cake on the way.'

We're halfway through the MathsQuest final – and it's going really well! We decided that as Polly is best at percentages and fractions, she does the buzzer for those questions and as I'm better at multiplying and dividing I'll do the buzzer for those. Anything else, we work out between us.

And it's worked! We have nine points. But so do William U and his teammate. William U's Maths has got five thousand per cent better (*not hyperbole*). They're obviously letting him inside the private school for his Maths lessons – he used to Find Maths a Challenge at St Lidwina's. It's just really annoying that William U's mum keeps coughing all the time. She's been doing it all afternoon. Her hay fever must be worse than William D's.

'Well, this is very exciting!' says Mr McHamm. 'I haven't been this nervous since I was cast as Back End of a Cow with Freddie "Farty" Fudgkins in the 1984 town panto!'

We're coming to the final question. I can feel the Worry Wobbles trying to take over. But I'm controlling them using my breathing. I look over at William U. He doesn't look worried at all. He looks really pleased with himself, which is weird, because we haven't even heard the question yet. 'With St Lidwina's Primary on nine points and Insufficient Prep on nine points, the MathsQuest champions will be decided by the final question.'

He leaves a big pause. William U's mum clears her throat. William U smiles.

'What is the square of fifteen?'

Polly and I grab our paper.

'OK – the square is fifteen times fifteen, so we need ten times fifteen ...'

William U's mum coughs. Then she coughs again.

'A hundred and fifty,' I say straight away.

William U's mum does another two coughs.

'Plus five times fifteen ...'

William U's mum coughs quickly five times. It's super distracting.

'Seventy-five,' I say, working it out quickly on

my paper.

'Add them together and the answer is ...'

William U's buzzer goes.

'Two hundred and twenty-five,' he says smugly. I look down at our paper. That's what I had written too.

'Is that your final answer?' says the Mayor. I think he's trying to be dramatic.

'It is,' says William U, looking at his grinning mum.

'Then I can tell you that you are ... CORRECT!' cries Mr McHamm, throwing his cards up in the air. 'The winners of MathsQuest are ... Insufficient Prep!'

I can't believe it. We lost. We lost to William U. I don't feel the Worry Wobbles. I feel like a big pile of manure.

Polly's hand reaches over to mine.

'Hey, we did really well,' she says. 'We nearly

beat them.'

'But we didn't,' I say as William U goes up to collect the MathsQuest trophy. I look into the audience, where Dad and Rita are sitting on different sides of the hall. They're both pretend-smiling and clapping at us. They look at each other. They both look really sad. But I don't think they're sad about MathsQuest.

'Well, it is my great privilege and honour,' says Mr McHamm, 'to declare the winner of MathsQuest—'

'STOP!' cries a voice at the back of the hall.

A man who had been sitting in a black cloak at

the back (*which I thought was a bit weird, by the way*) suddenly rips it off. It's Trent!

'I have an objection – no, an ACCUSATION!' Trent roars. 'Insufficient Prep have been CHEATING!'

The audience gasps. It's the most excited they've sounded all afternoon.

'That's a scandalous claim!' Mr McHamm huffs. 'I've not been this shocked since I was accused of tripping up TV's favourite interior design assistant Johnny Blashford so I could switch on the town Christmas lights myself! Where is your proof?'

'Here is my proof!' cries Trent, pulling out his phone. 'Insufficient Prep have been getting the answers fed to them all afternoon.'

'How?' shouts the Mayor. 'I've been watching them more closely than my university flatmate's acting career!'

'But have you been listening?' Trent asks, playing

223

a video. 'I think – no, I KNOW – that someone in the audience has been giving them the answers. Someone here has been COUGHING!'

He points at William U's mum, who is going very pink.

'I'll have you know I have Involuntary Tickling Lung Syndrome,' she says. 'I can't help but cough when I'm nervous.'

'Listen,' says Trent, playing the last question again. 'She has a system. Slow coughs for hundreds, faster ones for tens, quick ones for units. See?'

We listen to William U's mum cough the answer to the last question: 225.

'A coincidence,' laughs William U's mum.

'Do you want me to play you the cube of eight?' says Trent. 'The man next to you nearly called an ambulance.'

'Actually I was wiping the spit off my phone,' the man whispers.

'Is this true?' the Mayor asks.

'You don't understand,' mutters William U's mum. 'William has Winning Dependency Syndrome. He can't lose. He would have got the answers eventually. If My William loses he gets ... he gets ... he gets ... REALLY UPSET!'

'I'm sorry,' says Mr McHamm, 'but this is totally unacceptable! This is almost us unfair as when I was denied the lead role in *Cinderella*! Insufficient Prep School, I'm sorry to announce that you are disqualified!'

The Mayor goes to take the trophy back from William U. But William U won't let it go. Mr McHamm pulls it again, so William U pulls it back. Eventually, with a big tug, the Mayor wrestles it from William U's hands.

'MUUUUUUUUUMMMMMMM!' William U screams out.

William U's mum comes to the stage and guides

him quickly away.

'It's OK, William,' she whispers. 'I'll buy you your own trophy – a bigger trophy. And a football. And a pony ...'

I look into the audience where Dad is laughing so hard he is crying. Rita is cry-laughing too. They see each other and smile.

'Well now, in light of this ... development,' Mr McHamm announces. 'The *real* winner of this year's MathsQuest ... is St Lidwina's Primary School!'

'YEEEEEEESSSSSSSSSSS!' roars Trent, picking up his chair and smashing it on the floor. 'Yes! Yes! Yes!'

A security guard comes over.

'It's OK, I'm just leaving,' says our head teacher calmly, before walking out of the hall.

I can't believe it! We WON!

Polly and I have a massive hug and go to get our trophy.

'You take it,' says Polly. 'You got most of the answers right.'

'No – you take it,' I say to her. 'You stopped me from getting loads wrong.'

We smile and both put our hands on the trophy. We take it together and hold it up high.

Everyone claps and cheers. Dad is standing up and whooping so loudly I think he might be banned like Trent. Rita is on her feet too. Polly leans over to me.

'Scarlett?' she asks out of the corner of her mouth. 'Are you thinking what I'm thinking?'

I nod. And I don't think it's a coincidence this time.

'We are SO going to be Star of the Week this week,' I say.

'Not that,' smiles Polly. 'About my mum and your dad?'

I look at them both, smiling proudly at us.

We think it's time they went home in the same car.

CHAPTER √225

'Scarlett?' Dad says in the darkness. 'Scarlett? Where are you?'

Polly and I giggle from behind a bush deep in the gardens of Tottington Hall.

'Polly?' comes Rita's voice in the darkness. 'Polly – what is all this about? Oh ... hi, Bruce.'

'Rita,' says Dad, sounding happy. 'Do you know what's going on? I got a note to meet Scarlett here. Was this your idea?'

'No,' says Rita, holding up her identical note from Polly. She's smiling. And not a pretend smile. 'But I think I know whose it was.'

'Now!' I say to Polly, and she flicks the switch in her hand.

All the fairy lights light up around a picnic blanket, where Polly and I have made a feast for Dad and Rita.

'Wow,' says Dad, coming over to the blanket and looking at the food. 'Jam sandwiches ...'

'And ... salt and vinegar crisps,' says Rita. 'My favourite.'

(*Polly and I had to use what was in my cupboards, which wasn't very much, by the way.*)

'And what's this?' says Dad, picking the bottle out of the wine cooler. 'Oh my – it's the finest bottle of—'

'Blackcurrant cordial,' says Rita. 'What's going on?'

Polly nods at me and we come out from behind the bush.

'Hello, you pair,' says Dad. 'What are you up to?'

'We feel really bad,' says Polly. 'We're very sorry that we tried to split you up at Kamp KwalityTime.'

'Oh, girls,' says Rita. 'You don't have to explain. We completely—'

'Actually, yes we do,' I say, even though interrupting is a bit rude. 'We do need to explain.'

'Yes,' says Polly. 'We need to explain that we're really happy you've found each other.'

'And that we don't want you to break up,' I add.

'And that we know you've both been through

some really sad times, so we just want you to be happy,' says Polly.

'And that I'll be needing those crisps back 'cos they're for my packed lunch tomorrow,' I point out. (*They really are, by the way. I do want Dad and Rita to get back together. But I really like salt and vinegar crisps.*)

'But the main thing you need to know,' says Polly, taking my hand, 'is that Scarlett and I, well, we're ...'

'Friends now,' I say, smiling at Polly. 'Really good friends. And I really want you and Polly in my polygon. I liked being a square. But hexagons are really cool.'

I look at Rita. She is crying. My dad smiles at me, then takes her hand.

'Well,' he says. 'If the girls are happy ...'

'If you're both sure,' says Rita, not even really looking at us.

'We are,' we say, having a big hug.

Because we really are.

'Rita – I love you,' says Dad shyly.

'Bruce Fife – I'm crazy in love with you,' cries Rita, giving him a massive hug.

'Oh, Rita!'

'Oh, Bruce!'

'Oh, no!' say Polly and I as they have a massive fridgey kiss that lasts for ages.

'Well then,' says Dad, putting his arm round Rita. 'Let's tuck into our picnic.'

'Oh, it's not just a picnic,' Polly says quickly.

'No,' I add. 'We felt really bad that you missed the Fireworks Fiesta. So we asked Jakub for some help.'

'Hi, Bruce! Hi, Rita!' sobs Jakub from the other side of the garden. 'I'm so happy for you guys.'

(Jakub is really soppy, by the way – he cried at the end of UniMingoes 4Eva *when ShyMingo found*

her inner confidence and an exclusive UniMingoes
thermal water bottle.)

Jakub lights a match and a few seconds later a
beautiful firework erupts in the sky.

'Welcome to the Fireworks Fiesta!' Polly and I
say together.

'Oh – you girls,' says Rita, coming over and
giving us a big hug. 'You are the best.'

Dad comes over too and we all stand together
watching the beautiful colours light up the sky. I
have a feeling we'll all be going home in the same
car tonight.

'Ah – I almost forgot,' says Polly, pulling a piece
of paper out of her pocket. 'This is for you. We

wanted to give you the whole Kamp KwalityTime experience.'

She hands it over to Rita, who looks at it in confusion.

'What's this?' Dad asks.

Polly and I grin.

'The bill,' I tell him. 'That'll be £46.99, please ...'

CHAPTER 4²

Families aren't really like polygons at all.

Polygons have rules about their shape and size, but families can change shape and size all the time.

I thought my family was a square. But now it's a hexagon, with Rita and Polly in it. And when the snotty, farty baby comes, it'll be a heptagon.

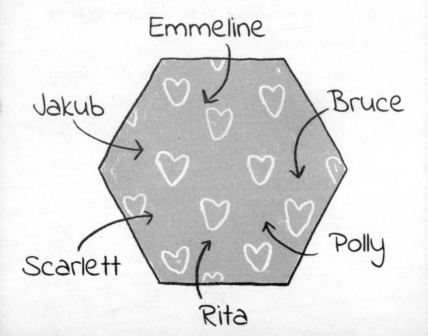

But then again, it was never really a square anyway, because my family has lots more people in it. There's Aunty Rosa and Aunty Amara and Granny. And then there's all the cousins on my granny's side that live in Wales (*the country, not the big mammal*) and all my dad's family and Jakub's family and now Rita and Polly's family. So I'm not going to worry too much about polygons any more. Perhaps we should be more like head teachers. Those change all the time. (*Trent has left St Lidwina's, by the way. He said he was sorry – no, DEVASTATED – but he needed a new challenge. So he's retraining to be an Olympic wrestler.*)

It's Easter Day and we're all at the hospital together. Granny has had her operation and she's feeling much better. She can't come home yet, so we've all come to her with Easter eggs and cakes and presents. I brought the MathsQuest trophy to show her and she's super proud of me (*later on at our sleepover at her house, Polly and I are going to fill our trophy with popcorn while we watch* UniMingoes 2 *in her new bunk beds, by the way*). And I'm super proud of Granny for having her operation. But I won't fill her with popcorn.

'Please may I have an apple juice?' I ask.

'I think you've had enough sugar for one day,' says Mum, giving me a cuddle.

'But it isn't sugar,' I point out. 'It's a wet apple. In a glass.'

'Scarlett, just stick to water,' says Mum.

'But, Mum ...'

'Um ... everyone? We have an announcement,' says Aunty Rosa, holding Aunty Amara's hand.

'Oh – so do we,' says Mum.

Uh-oh. Here we go again.

I feel the Worry Wobbles start again. What now?

'You go first,' says Aunty Rosa.

'No – you were first,' says Mum.

'It's fine – after you.'

'No – I'll wait for you.'

'But I want to know what you're going to say.'

'And I'll tell you after I've heard your news.'

'But I want—'

'GIRLS!' snaps Granny. Phew. The operation hasn't taken her formidable out. 'Rosa, let's hear your news. Then you, Emmeline.'

Oooh. Granny used Mum's big name. She's in trouble. And, looking at her grumpy face, she knows it.

'OK ... so we've been doing a lot of thinking about our move to America,' Aunty Rosa says. 'And we decided that ...'

Oh no. They're going to move further away? To Africa? To Australia? To the moon?

'... it's not the right time,' Aunty Rosa continues.

'In fact, we don't think it'll ever be the right time,' smiles Aunty Amara. 'We love you all so much. We don't want to be on the other side of the world.'

'And so,' Aunty Rosa starts.

'And so,' Aunty Amara continues.

They look at each other and smile.

'WE'RE STAYING HERE!' they cheer.
AAAAARRRRRGGGGGHHHHH!

That's the BEST NEWS EVER!! We all put down our cake and Easter eggs (*after one last bite*) and go and hug Aunty Rosa and Aunty Amara because we're all so relieved that they're staying. Granny looks super happy as Aunty Rosa goes and gives her a big kiss.

'But what about your big adventure?' Granny asks her.

'Look at us!' Aunty Rosa grins. 'I think there are plenty of big adventures for us to have right here.'

I look around my polygon. Yes, I think there are lots of adventures for us to have. Some will be good and some will be scary. But with my whole family here to help me, perhaps I don't need to worry so much.

'So,' says Mum quietly. 'We've got an announcement too.'

She looks at Jakub and then looks at me.

'We had a scan to check the baby ...'

'Are you all right?' says Granny, looking worried. 'Is the baby all right?'

I feel another Worry Wobble start. I might not want the snotty, farty baby in my bedroom. But I want it to be OK.

'I'm absolutely fine,' smiles Mum. 'And the baby's fine too. In fact ... both the babies are fine ...'

Everyone gasps and starts laughing. I don't understand. What other baby?

'I don't understand? What other baby?' I ask, because I don't understand what other baby they're talking about.

'Scarlett,' says Mum, coming and holding my hands. 'I'm going to have twins.'

WHAT???!!!

TWO SNOTTY, FARTY BABIES???!!!

THAT ONLY LEAVES TWO BEDROOMS

FOR ME!!!

I can feel the BIG (Angry) FEELINGS start to boil in my tummy. I'm not happy about this at all.

'Hi, Mrs Andrews,' says the nice nurse called Freda. She's pushing a trolley (*a hospital trolley, not a supermarket trolley*) that's covered in bags that look like they're full of apple juice. I look at the trolley with a tummy full of BIG (Angry) FEELINGS. 'I've just come to change your bag.'

(*Granny can't get out of bed to go to the toilet, so she has a special tube to help her Spend a Penny in a bag under her bed, by the way.*)

Freda picks up Granny's bag and puts it on her trolley. But I'm still thinking about TWO snotty, farty babies, who are DEFINITELY going to be seen AND heard when we move to Tottington Hall and then the dragon will come and find us and turn us all to cat ash and no one asked me about any of this and I'm starting to feel very angry and like

243

something's going to explode again ...

I try to focus on the bags, which are fizzing and wobbling as Freda starts to push her trolley. I don't want to make a scene like I did the time we were in A Posh Restaurant and my chicken had gravy all over it, even though I'd asked not to have it and I got BIG (Angry) FEELINGS and exploded gravy all over the waiter and oh no, I think it's happening again and it's not apple juice in those bags, but I can't stop it because those bags are about to go ...

KER-SPLASH!

Uh-oh.

On second thoughts, I think I will stick to water.

ACKNOWLEDGEMENTS

One of the loveliest things about writing Scarlett's stories is that I don't get any Worry Wobbles about them – and that's because, like Scarlett, I'm surrounded by people who really help me. Front of the line is my brilliant editor, Rachel Wade, who has been such a superstar over this past wobbly year and I can't thank her enough for all she has done for me. Veronique B, Alison P, Emily T, Emily F and everyone at Hachette – thank you too for all your hard work getting Scarlett out into the world. #TeamScarlett is an explosive force indeed.

I must give a double enormo-thanks (because I didn't do it last time and I'm a wally) to Chris Jevons, whose brilliant illustrations bring

245

Scarlett to life in a way my stick-men just never could. It's been a joy working with you, Chris and thank you for your supreme talent and not batting an eyelid at whatever strange creation I have thrown your way. UniMingoes Forever...

This book is dedicated to my best friend Martha, 'Arf', Bachle-Morris, who has been my BFF for (say it quickly) nearly 30 years. Like Maisie, Arf always gives me invaluable perspective (even though she wears contact lenses, not red glasses) and makes me laugh so hard I fart a bit. I love you so much, Arf – thank you for only ever making me wobbly in the funnest of ways.

To my family – I love you harder than ever. Thank you, thank you, thank you for unwobbling me every day.

And to my wonderful readers – your lovely response to *The Exploding Life of Scarlett Fife* has given me very BIG FEELINGS, but all of them are smiley happy ones. I hope you've enjoyed Scarlett's latest adventure – there will be another one with you before you can say, 'Number Two',

Sending you all my love,
Maz
xxx

LOOK OUT FOR SCARLETT'S OTHER STORIES